CLEARWATER JUSTICE

For five long years Deputy Jim Lawson has wanted to find the man who murdered his brother Benny. So when prime suspect Tyler Coleman rides into Clearwater, Jim slaps him in jail. But almost immediately the only witness to the appalling crime turns up dead and the outlaw Luther Wade rides into town and vows to break Tyler out of jail by sundown.

Then Jim's investigation takes an unexpected twist when he finds evidence linking Benny's murder to the disappearance of the beguiling Zelma Hayden, the woman he had once hoped to marry.

Can Jim uncover the truth before the many guns lining up against him deliver their own justice?

D0943492

CLEARWATER JUSTICE

SCOTT CONNOR

 CULBIN PRESS

Names, characters and incidents in this book are fictional, and any resemblance to actual events, locales, organizations, or persons living or dead, is purely coincidental.

First published in 2005 by Robert Hale Limited
Copyright © 2005, 2014, 2016 by Scott Connor
ISBN: 9798595741705

All rights reserved.
No part of this book may be reproduced, or stored in a retrieval system, or transmitted in any form or by any means, electronic, mechanical, photocopying, recording, or otherwise, without express written permission of the author.

Published by Culbin Press.

ONE

When Sheriff Cliff Hopeman showed two fingers, Deputy Jim Lawson faced the door. When Hopeman showed one finger, Jim slipped his Peacemaker from its holster and when Hopeman lowered that finger, Jim kicked open the door.

The door slammed back against the wall, but before it could rebound, Jim hurried into the hotel room with Hopeman at his heels. Inside, two men stood by a table, a third man sat at the table and all were packing guns.

As Hopeman and Jim skidded to a halt both the standing men threw their hands to their holsters, but Hopeman ripped lead into the man on the left's guts, dropping him. Jim thundered a high slug into the man on the right's chest, which made him stagger backward before he crashed into the wall.

A second slug ensured he was dead before he hit the floor. Then Hopeman and Jim stood side by side, their guns trained on the sitting man.

"Reach, or die," Jim said.

The man at the table snorted. "You can't burst in here making demands and shooting up—"

"I'm Deputy Lawson and this is Sheriff Hopeman." Jim rolled his shoulders. "You just made a big mistake returning to our town, Tyler Coleman."

The man chuckled, nothing in his calm demeanor suggesting that Jim's identification was correct, but his eyes gleamed, perhaps with real humor.

"You've got the wrong man." He placed his hands on the table and clasped them. "So, leave."

"I reckon I'm right. So you'll come with

us." Jim edged a pace to the side, leaving a clear route to the door.

The man slid his hands to the edge of the table. He rocked forward, moving as if to rise, and then slumped back into his chair and rested his hands on his lap.

"I assume that once I've proved who I am and that I'm not this Tyler Coleman, you'll release me."

"*If* I've made a mistake, you can go, but now, you've got a choice – come with me and get the court's justice." Jim raised his Peacemaker to sight the man's forehead. "Or stay sitting and get my justice."

The man leaned forward and rocked his head from side to side, but then twitched. Hot fire thundered up through the table as he ripped lead at the deputy from a concealed weapon. Splinters flew as the slug hurtled by Jim's ear and blasted into the ceiling.

Jim leaped to the side, saving himself from a second slug. Hopeman tore off a wild shot as the man kicked out. The toe of the man's boot hit the table and knocked it up into Hopeman's face, forcing the sheriff to waste another shot, firing blind.

As Hopeman extricated himself from the furniture, the man rose to his feet and aimed his gun at the sprawling deputy. In desperation, Hopeman lunged for his arm and thrust it high. They struggled, both men straining to turn the derringer on the other man.

Their mutual grip around the gun fired another slug into the ceiling, but by then Jim was on his feet. He waited for an opening and, when the man pushed Hopeman away, he sent him sprawling with a solid blow to the chin.

Even as the man was sliding to a halt, Jim was on him. He kicked his gun away, hoisted him up by the collar and thrust the barrel of his gun right between his eyes.

"Assaulting a lawman is another charge I can add to the list, Tyler," he said.

Even though the barrel forced the man's head back, he ignored the gun, his eyes only for the deputy.

"If you're so sure of who I am, shoot me."

Jim snorted and dragged him up to a sitting position.

"I'm not doing that. I reckon everyone in Clearwater should get a chance to see you swing."

Hopeman yanked the man's arms back and secured him in handcuffs. Then, while he pulled their prisoner to his feet, Jim checked that the other men in the room were, in fact, dead. He turned to the window.

Outside, passersby had stopped and were facing the hotel, but Jim didn't acknowledge them and went to the door. He checked that the corridor was clear. Then, five paces ahead of Hopeman and their prisoner, he left the hotel room and walked down the stairs into the Rusty Spur saloon.

As Jim expected, the gunfire had silenced the saloon's normally boisterous evening crowd. Now the customers lined the bar, facing the stairs and regarding the three descending men with the wide-eyed bemusement that greeted the rare trouble that came Clearwater's way.

At the end of the bar, Max Malloy muttered an oath and tipped back his hat. The people around him turned to ask what had surprised him, but Max's mouth just fell open. He barged the men surrounding him aside and dashed outside, calling out the news.

So by the time Jim pushed the batwings apart all the people who had been on the main drag were milling in front of the saloon and eager to find out if Max was right. The gathering crowd parted as Hopeman dragged their uncomplaining prisoner to the sheriff's office.

From the mutterings and the shaking heads, many of the people in the crowd, like Max, had recognized their prisoner. As always, the undertaker, Gene Trentham, was waiting on the boardwalk outside the office, but for once his tall hat wasn't set at a jaunty angle in anticipation of business.

"Start smiling, Gene," Hopeman said as Deputy Newell came out of the office and opened the door for him. "You've got two customers back in the Rusty Spur, and this one will need your services soon."

Gene flashed a wan smile, and then lowered his head.

"I've got more business than just that," he said. "Monty Elwood is dead."

With just a raised eyebrow, Hopeman ordered Jim to deal with this, and then dragged the prisoner into the sheriff's office.

"How did he die?" Jim asked as the sheriff kicked the door shut behind him.

Gene hunched over, wringing his hands. A sigh escaped his lips as he shuffled around on the spot, and then led Jim through the thronging crowd and back across the main drag.

"It isn't much of a sight," he said. "He put a shotgun to his head."

Jim snorted a humorless chuckle. "I'm surprised his aim was good enough to hit anything he shot at."

Gene returned an agreeing snort. "Yeah, but from the empty whiskey bottle by his body, I reckon he was just drunk enough to kill himself, and just sober enough to do it right."

"You found him?"

"Yeah." Gene stopped on the boardwalk outside Monty's rundown store. "I heard the gunfire in the Rusty Spur and came to see what was happening, but then heard another gunshot in his store. So I looked in on him, and. . . ."

Jim rubbed his chin. "Had you seen him earlier?"

"Yeah, in the Rusty Spur. He was his usual self." Gene frowned. "What are you thinking?"

"I'm just wondering if he'd seen that Tyler Coleman was back in town."

Gene nodded as he pushed the door open. "I guess that would have been enough to make him kill himself."

Outside the sheriff's office the townsfolk were now five deep around the windows and door, and craning their necks in hope of catching sight of the prisoner. He shrugged and then headed inside after Gene and walked across the store.

A smear of blood, a shotgun and an empty whiskey bottle on the counter heralded what was there, but Jim still took a deep breath before he approached the counter. Monty lay sprawled on the floor on the other side, his lower leg bent and to the side, a hand outstretched as if reaching for something.

The thick pool of blood surrounding his head and the wasted remnants of his face said that he'd never reach whatever it was he was grasping for. Jim and Gene stood with their heads bowed.

Then Jim slipped behind the counter and stood over the body. He faced the door. The shotgun was at his right hand, the barrels aiming toward the door, and the whiskey bottle was at his left hand.

He mimed taking the gun in hand, holding the barrels right between his eyes and pulling the trigger. He staggered back, and then stood aside to examine the body again. He judged that if Monty had shot himself, he would have fallen in the place where the body was now lying, and the shock would have driven the shotgun from his hand to let it spin to a halt on the counter.

He stepped over the body and came out from behind the counter. More spots of blood were on the counter and even on the floor beyond.

"Are you worried this wasn't suicide?" Gene asked.

Jim kneeled to finger one of the blood spots and shook his head.

"When this happened, our prisoner was being arrested, but as we can't ask Monty whether he saw Tyler before he killed himself, I'll note that he probably did, and put this death down as being Tyler's last victim."

Gene nodded and together, they left the store. In silence, they parted and, as Gene headed to his workshop, Jim returned to the sheriff's office. In the last five minutes the crowd had doubled in size.

Everyone who had been in the Rusty Spur had joined the others in a vigil outside the office. As yet, the low conversation was more excited than annoyed as everyone shared the snippets of information they'd gathered.

Jim didn't expect the cheerful attitude to last for long. He fought a path through the crowd, refusing all demands to add more details or confirm that the man they had arrested was, in fact, Tyler Coleman.

Nobody asked him about Monty Elwood. Inside the office, he relayed the circumstances of Monty's death to Hopeman, receiving frequent sad shakes of the head from Hopeman in acknowledgment of the death of Clearwater's least reputable citizen.

A firm and steady knock at the door halted Jim's tale. They turned to the window, where outside, the crowd milled in, pressing their faces to the window. One gaunt and tall man stood out from the rabble.

Everyone gave this man a wide berth,

suggesting he was generating his own zone of quiet despair as he looked through the window in the door, his deep-set eyes lost to a sorrow that time could never heal.

"Caleb Lawson," Hopeman said.

Jim sighed. "I guessed it wouldn't be long before the news of Tyler's arrest spread to my father. Shall I let him in?"

Hopeman sighed and slapped his legs. "Yeah. At the very least, we'll get an official identification."

Jim nodded and opened the door. He stood before the doorway, his hands raised to grip the doorframe.

"Pa, I'm obliged that you came," he said.

Caleb raised his chin, his back as straight as always, his eyes as cold as they had been for the last five years.

"I had to, now you've finally got the man who shot our Benny," he said, his jaw set fit to burst.

"I hope it's him, but you can tell us for sure, if you can cope."

"I can," Caleb said. "Stand aside."

Jim kept a hand on the doorframe, blocking Caleb's route into the office. He held out his other hand and pointed at Caleb's gunbelt.

"I will, but only when I have your gun."

Caleb placed his hands on his hips. "I won't shoot that snake. I want to savior the moment when the law finally delivers justice and he swings."

"I know, Pa. That's why we took him alive." Jim flashed a smile. "But you will give me your gun."

"Your mother would never have accepting your treating me like that." Caleb's jaw muscles rippled, but with a lunge, he unhooked his gunbelt and thrust it into Jim's hand. "Now will you trust me?"

Jim rocked back to throw the belt on his desk. He decided that as he'd already insulted his father more than he deserved, he wouldn't make it worse by frisking him for a hidden weapon, so he stood aside and directed him to the corner cell.

Caleb received a ripple of dignified

encouragement from the nearest people surrounding the door, as he headed inside. Several people tried to follow him in, but Jim stood in front of the door.

With a few polite pushes, he removed them from the office and closed the door. Caleb stomped to a halt and faced the corner cell. For long moments, the office was quiet. The prisoner sat on his cot, facing Caleb through the bars, and Deputy Newell and Sheriff Hopeman stood on either side of Caleb, as he snorted long breaths through his nostrils, his eyes wide and blank.

Hopeman gestured to Jim and to the windows. Seeing his concern, Jim closed the shutters, cutting off the view of the people outside of an encounter that nobody in Clearwater ever expected to happen.

Jim's bustling activity broke Caleb's catatonic spell. He strode toward the cell and swung to a halt at arm's length from the bars.

"I've got to ask you, is that him?" Hopeman said.

Caleb closed his eyes and gripped his hands so tightly all color drained from them. Then Hopeman strode across the room and laid a hand on Caleb's shoulder. This encouraged Caleb to open his eyes.

"That's Tyler Coleman, the man who shot my son," he said, his voice a strangulated whisper.

Inside the cell the prisoner uttered a snort, but Hopeman patted Caleb's shoulder and gently directed him away from the cell.

"I'll need more from you later, but for now you can rest easy. It's over."

Caleb pushed Hopeman away from him to stand clear and, with a trembling finger, pointed into the cell.

"It isn't over." Caleb raised his hand and rubbed it over his face, stilling the shaking, his expression now more tired than shocked. "I won't rest easy until he swings."

Hopeman nodded and stood aside, letting Caleb walk away. In front of the door, Caleb stopped and held out his hand. Jim took the gunbelt from the desk and slapped it into

Caleb's palm.

Caleb reached for the door, but then turned around. The prisoner had rolled from his cot and stood up. He'd thrown up both hands to hold the bars and pressed his face between them. He licked his lips and grinned.

Caleb's shoulders shook. His lips trembled as a solitary tear fell from his right eye. With a huge roar, he aimed his gun while it was still in the holster at Tyler, so Jim lunged to the side to knock Caleb's arm up as he fired.

Lead blasted through the bottom of the holster, but it clattered into the cell bars, a foot above Tyler's head. As the slug ricocheted away, Tyler leaped for cover beneath his cot. Jim grabbed Caleb's arm and held it high, and Hopeman prized the gun and gunbelt from his slack fingers.

"Pa, that wasn't the way," Jim said.

"It's the only way that snake will understand," Caleb said.

Caleb flexed his shoulders and tried to push Jim and Hopeman away from him, but the lawmen had a firm grip of his arms and turned him around and to the door.

"Hey, I want to press charges," Tyler whined, from under his cot. "He tried to kill me."

"Be quiet, Tyler," Hopeman shouted over his shoulder.

Deputy Newell opened the door. Outside, the crowd pressed in, but when Jim maneuvered Caleb outside, Gene slipped through the people. A wan smile from Jim was all the explanation Gene needed as he led Caleb away.

Jim stood in the doorway. His firm-jawed stance encouraged the crowd to break up and wander back to their former business, shaking their heads. He returned to the office, locked the door and joined Hopeman and Newell in sitting at his desk in anticipation of what he was sure would be a long vigil.

"I don't want you to go thinking I'm not obliged, Deputy," Tyler said from his cell. "You just saved my life."

"Only so you can swing," Jim said.

"I wouldn't be so sure of that." Tyler chuckled and rolled on to his cot. "I reckon you'll live just long enough to regret that mistake."

TWO

"Do you reckon anyone else will come?" Jim asked.

Gene patted Monty Elwood's coffin. "I doubt it."

Gene had set out two rows of chairs, but the two lawmen were the only people who had come to pay their respects. They both sighed and removed their hats. It had been two days since they'd captured Tyler Coleman.

Tyler's murder of Benny Lawson five years earlier was still an open sore for many. So in case anyone else decided to deliver justice to Clearwater's most notorious wanted man before Judge Plummer could come from Green Valley, Hopeman and his deputies had remained on constant guard, but after Caleb's sudden action, nobody had tried anything.

Even so, there was a constant bustle of people outside the office, each person eager to catch sight of the prisoner. With all that activity, the funeral of Monty Elwood had just been forgotten. In the quiet part of the afternoon Hopeman had left Deputy Newell in charge of guarding Tyler for an hour so the two lawmen could attend the burial.

"Father Stanton must be coming, surely?" Hopeman asked, pointing at the unoccupied chairs. "He officiated over the burial of those two hired guns."

Gene shook his head. "He isn't coming either. Ever since Monty stole Stanton's cross and tried to sell it in his store, he's never forgiven him."

Hopeman blew out his cheeks. "Well, if we haven't got a man of the cloth to say a few words, what do we do?"

"Monty wouldn't have wanted any Bible words uttered over his body, but I guess one of us ought to say something about him."

Hopeman snorted so Jim took a deep breath and stood up. Gene made way for him to stand by the coffin. The deputy rocked his head from side to side, and then turned to Gene and Hopeman.

"Monty Elwood was. . . ." Jim shrugged and rubbed his chin. "He was . . . He was a man."

Hopeman chuckled. "You've got to say more than that."

Jim slapped the coffin lid. "Then I'll say this: he enjoyed life. He always had a kind word to say to you, and no matter how much mischief he caused, he never pushed things too far. So I'll remember him as a decent citizen of Clearwater."

For long moments silence reigned.

"Who are you talking about now?" Hopeman asked.

"Monty, he. . . ." Jim sighed on seeing that Hopeman was smiling.

"Sheriff, a man is dead," Gene said. "Even if that man is Monty Elwood, we must pay him some respect."

"The only respect I can pay the likes of Monty is that Clearwater will be quieter without him. You can take that any way you want." Hopeman swung his hat on to his head and stood up. "Anybody else want to say something before we plant him in a hole?"

"I do," a voice intoned from the doorway.

Everyone turned to the door where a burly man was filling the doorway. A thick red beard covered his face almost up to the sharp eyes that were sizing up the few occupants within moments.

"Who are you?" Hopeman asked.

With slow paces the man strode into the room and stomped to a halt. He removed his hat and batted the trail dust to the floor against his thigh, and then ruffled his buffalo-hide jacket.

"The name's Armstrong McGiven and I knew Monty." He closed his eyes for a moment. His lips mouthed something, perhaps a silent prayer. Then he strode across the room to stand beside the coffin. "How did he die?"

"He shot himself," Gene said.

Armstrong lowered his head. "That isn't any kind of death for a man like Monty."

"I guess you're right," Hopeman said. He raised his eyebrows, and both men returned a bemused shrug.

Armstrong reached out to remove the coffin lid, but Gene placed a hand on his arm.

"It's a mighty bad sight," Gene said. "He aimed real well."

"I've seen dead men before." Armstrong swung the lid away. He winced.

"I told you it was—"

"I'm not concerned about the sight. It's the smell."

Gene leaned over the coffin and sniffed. "Monty doesn't smell much worse dead than alive."

Armstrong swung the lid back on the coffin. "Then clean him up."

"I don't see why. . . ."

Gene turned to Hopeman for support, but Armstrong extracted a wad of bills from his pocket, peeled off a ten-dollar bill and passed it to Gene.

"A man like Monty shouldn't be buried in those rags. He deserves to meet his maker in his best."

"Those clothes *were* his best."

"Then get some decent clothes on him," Armstrong snapped, and then softened his voice. "Get him cleaned up. Then I'll bury him with dignity."

Gene nodded. He held his hands before him and bowed his head.

"I'll see to it."

Armstrong turned and walked across the room and, without even acknowledging the two lawmen, departed from the undertaker's workshop.

"Now that was unexpected," Hopeman said.

Jim stood up. "It makes me wonder whether we misjudged Monty. He couldn't have always been a whiskey hound."

Hopeman grunted his disbelief, but Jim left the workshop, thoughtfully rubbing his chin. Monty's friend was walking toward the Rusty Spur, his gait purposeful. Hopeman joined Jim and, with Clearwater being quiet this afternoon, encouraged him to find out how Armstrong had come to know Monty.

So while Hopeman returned to the sheriff's office to resume his guarding of Tyler, Jim followed Armstrong down the main drag and into the saloon. At the bar he stood beside Armstrong and although Armstrong didn't acknowledge him he attracted the bartender's attention first and ordered two whiskeys.

"I'm obliged," Armstrong said. He pushed Jim's money aside and threw some coins on the table. "But I'll pay. Monty wouldn't have wanted me to do anything else."

Jim nodded and pocketed the coins. Jim's drink arrived and he swirled the whiskey in the glass before taking a gulp.

"You speak well of him. How did you know him?"

"We rode together some years back." Armstrong knocked back half his drink and placed the glass back on the bar. "I saw him from time to time since, but I hadn't realized that. . . ."

Armstrong frowned, the sun-baked wrinkles around his eyes ridging.

"That he'd fallen so far?"

"Yeah. I thought the whole town would have turned out to mourn the passing of such a great man." Armstrong cocked his ear to listen to the hubbub of chatter. "I never expected everyone to be talking about a lowdown outlaw and that the only people to attend his funeral would be the people who had to attend."

"I didn't have to. Monty didn't worry me as much as he annoyed others."

"I'm glad to hear it." Armstrong leaned on the bar and sipped his whiskey.

Jim sipped his drink and sighed. "It's a pity you couldn't have arrived a few days earlier. Meeting an old friend might have persuaded Monty to avoid doing what he did."

"Perhaps you're right, but Monty always knew his own mind. If he'd decided to kill himself, he'd do it no matter what anyone said."

Jim shrugged. "The Monty you talk about doesn't sound like the man everyone in Clearwater knew. If you're staying in town after you've buried him, I'd appreciate hearing about a different side to him."

Armstrong lowered his glass, and then poured himself and Jim another whiskey.

"As long as tales are still told about a man, that man isn't really dead, but I can't." He sighed. "I'm moving on once I've buried Monty."

For a few minutes they stood in companionable silence, but with their conversation ending, Max Malloy sidled down the bar with a lively grin on his face.

"You're here to bury Monty, you say?" he asked.

Jim raised a warning hand to Max, but Armstrong was already turning his head to him.

"I am."

"That's good," Max said. He licked his lips. "I just hope the worms don't get so annoyed with the smell that they throw him back."

As Max's two drinking companions, Channing and Grange, guffawed at Max's poor attempt at wit, Armstrong placed his glass on the bar and swung around to confront Max.

"Monty was the best shot, the bravest man and the finest friend any man could want. You'll take that back, or I'll pound your head into the wall until something gives."

Max gulped, but Channing and Grange muttered an oath and strode down the bar to flank him. With their encouraging presence, Max stood tall.

"I'm not taking anything back about the likes of Monty."

Armstrong rolled his shoulders, but Jim slapped a firm hand on his arm.

"Deputy, you can't stop me from defending my friend's good name," Armstrong said.

"I wasn't," Jim said. "I was offering to help you."

"I'm obliged for the offer, but I don't need no help to deal with these men."

Max grunted his irritation and, with Channing and Grange goading him on, took a long pace toward Armstrong and hurled a flailing blow at his face. Armstrong swayed back from the blow and thudded a short-arm jab into Max's guts that bent him double.

As Max gasped for air, Armstrong grabbed his shoulders, turned him around and kicked him toward his companions. Grange stepped back, standing tall by the bar, and Max stumbled by him to crash into Channing.

The entangled men tumbled to the floor. As the men floundered Grange turned, but walked into Armstrong's pile-driving blow to the jaw. His head cracked back as he toppled into the bar, and a second back-handed slap almost knocked him to his knees, only a sharp uppercut to his chin stopping him from falling.

A solid slug to the cheek wheeled him over the bar. As Grange clattered to the floor, Armstrong batted his hands together, but before he could turn, Channing extricated himself from Max.

He rolled to his feet and jumped on Armstrong's back. Then he wrapped both hands around his chin and tried to yank his head back. Armstrong merely dropped to his knees and thrust his head down to hurl Channing over his shoulders.

Channing somersaulted before he landed flat on his back. He sat up to meet a round-footed kick to the chin that pole-axed him in a moment. Armstrong stood tall. He turned, took hold of Max's collar and pulled him up to his chin.

"Now, it's your turn," he said, smiling. "Do you want driven through the wall, or do you want to tell me what you really think of Monty?"

"Monty was a. . . ." Max sighed and

slumped his shoulders. "He was a great man."

Armstrong nodded and moved to kick Max a pace toward the door, but Jim pushed himself from the bar to stand beside them.

"That's enough," he said. "You've won this fight and now you've got no reason to kick Monty out of the saloon."

"Please accept my apologies, Deputy," Armstrong said with a begrudging nod. Then, with a snap of his wrist, he released Max's collar.

Jim nodded. He took hold of Max's jacket and marched him to the door. With a firm lunge he hurled him through the batwings. As Max rolled off the boardwalk to lie on his back on the hardpan, he returned to the bar.

"Apology accepted," he said. "Just remember it's my job to throw his sort out of saloons."

Armstrong nodded his approval while filling Jim's half-full whiskey glass. Jim raised the glass to his lips, but then noticed that the hubbub of chatter in the saloon hadn't returned. As he lowered the glass, the doors creaked and footfalls stomped into the saloon.

Jim expected that Max had returned to escalate his fight, but the newcomer was a man he hadn't seen for five years, Luther Wade. The squat man stood with a hand on each batwing with his hat cocked low.

Out on the boardwalk, three other men flanked him. When Luther faced Jim, a sneering snort escaped his thin lips. Then, to his beckoning wave, all four men swaggered into the saloon and straight toward Jim.

THREE

The men brushed past Jim and lined up at the bar beside him. Jim turned and fingered his glass, but when the bartender provided the newcomers with whiskeys, Jim felt the back of his neck burn. He still stayed hunched, but when the feeling refused to go away, with a deliberate swing of the head, he turned to find Luther Wade was facing him.

Jim tipped back his hat. "Do you want me?"

"Yeah," Luther said through clenched teeth. "I was heading to the sheriff's office to give Sheriff Hopeman a message, but you can save me a journey. He'll release Tyler Coleman by sundown, if he doesn't want trouble."

Jim pushed himself away from the bar and turned around to confront Luther.

"A man who provides messages like that is looking to join Tyler in a cell."

Luther shrugged and hunched over the bar. Beside him, the other three men drank their whiskeys with the studied intensity of men who were making a show of ignoring this conversation. Luther raised his glass to his lips, but then lowered it.

"I haven't done nothing wrong, Deputy."

"Yet, but words are easy," Jim said, squaring off to Luther. "Have you got the guts to deliver more?"

Luther fingered his glass and then pushed it away from him, swirling the liquid across the bar. He snorted and took a steady pace toward Jim.

"I'll bide my time, but if Tyler is still in a cell at sundown, I'll do what I have to do."

Jim bent at the waist to thrust his face into Luther's face, their noses just inches apart.

"Now that was a threat, and men who

make threats end up in a cell."

With his index finger, Luther tipped his hat back on his head, and then patted that finger against his bristled chin as he backed away a pace, a smile twitching his lips. He bunched a fist, but when Jim chuckled he slackened his hand and turned around to move toward the door.

Then he snapped back, his hand whirling to his holster. Jim had anticipated Luther's action and went for his gun, but Armstrong lunged out from the bar and grabbed Luther's wrist as the fingers brushed the stock. He pulled the hand high.

"Run along like the deputy told you," he said, thrusting the arm up Luther's back and spinning him around.

The men at the bar edged back a pace, their hands twitching toward their gunbelts, but a shake of the head from Luther made them raise their hands. Armstrong held on to Luther, but when Luther grunted an oath, he thrust his arm up so that Luther had to stand on tiptoes, and then pushed him toward the door.

Luther stumbled to a halt, but he remained facing the door. With a roll of the shoulders and a smoothing of his jacket, he walked across the saloon. A short wave encouraged the other men to peel away from the bar.

With Luther at the back, the men strode to the saloon door, each pace slow and deliberate. Luther stopped in the doorway.

"I'm leaving only because I chose to," he said. "Next time, I'll leave with Tyler."

Then, with a mocking tip of his hat, Luther walked through the batwings and outside.

* * *

"We've got trouble," Jim said as he walked into the sheriff's office. "Luther Wade is back in town."

"Who's he?" Newell asked.

"He roared through Clearwater with Tyler," Hopeman said. "Tyler had the brains while Luther had the gun. Where did you see him?"

"He was in the saloon with three other hard-cases threatening to break Tyler out of jail by sundown."

In the corner cell Tyler was just as morose as he had been since they'd arrested him, but Hopeman still drew Jim to the window and out of Tyler's earshot.

"Luther will have more men with him than that." Hopeman shrugged. "But I'm comforted to know Tyler's friend is worried he'll be found guilty."

"What do you mean?"

Hopeman lowered his voice. "Judge Plummer should be here within the week for Tyler's trial, but I'm worried what'll happen then. I've been pulling together the evidence and I've got to admit there's no real proof that Tyler killed your brother."

"But he did," Jim snapped.

"I know, but Monty was the only witness."

Jim tipped back his hat. "Are you saying someone killed Monty to stop him testifying? Because it looked to me like he killed himself."

"I don't know what to believe. Gene is the only one who's sure he heard a gunshot in Monty's store. Some reckon they might have heard a shot an hour earlier, but. . . ."

"That isn't enough to doubt anything."

"It isn't." Hopeman walked around on the spot, tapping a fist against his thigh. "There's more happening here than I first thought. I've alerted Marshal Kirby, but as I don't want to call him in, it's time we found some real proof."

* * *

Jim stood in the doorway to Monty's store, his lip curled with distaste. With Jim's interest in forming a case against Tyler being so personal, Sheriff Hopeman had let him take control of the investigation, and his first discovery was that someone had ransacked the place.

After the saloon fight, he assumed that it

was Max Malloy and, from the systematic nature of the destruction, he reckoned Max was searching for something. So Jim left the store and asked around, learning that Max had hurried out of town, heading west toward Black Pass.

This was just too much of a coincidence, so, at a gallop, Jim rode out of Clearwater, while keeping on the look-out for Luther. Only when he closed on the small rounded hill at the intersection of the trails north and west did he notice the first movement out on the trail.

He narrowed his eyes and confirmed that it was just Gene Trentham's wagon. Riding up front with Gene was Armstrong McGiven and on the back sat a simple wooden coffin. Jim slowed to avoid disrupting their dignified journey to the town cemetery, but with the wagon traveling slowly, Jim had no choice but to be just a few dozen yards behind them when the wagon pulled up.

Gene and Armstrong alighted and slid the coffin from the back of the wagon. Gene nodded toward him, but Armstrong ignored him. Jim waited until they were walking up the hill and then hurried his horse on, but as he passed the wagon, he slowed to a halt.

His journey was pressing, but after being a party to the rude way they'd dealt with Monty's funeral earlier today, he decided to make amends by paying his respects properly. Still, he didn't join them, but dismounted and stood at the base of the hill.

He removed his hat as Armstrong and Gene carried the coffin to the brow of the hill. They lowered the coffin into the ground and immediately Gene turned and headed down the hill, leaving Armstrong to cover the hole with rocks on his own. Gene smiled at Jim as he passed and confirmed he would be welcome, so he walked up the hill and joined Armstrong.

"This is a good place," he said, halting ten yards back from Armstrong. "When you've gone, I'll pass by and tend Monty's grave."

Armstrong set his jaw firm. "Why?"

Jim opened his mouth, but then closed it.

He rejected several answers before settling for the truth.

"You stood by me in the saloon when Luther was getting gun-crazy, and my mother and Benny are buried just down the hill, so it's no trouble."

Armstrong shrugged. "I don't want you helping if you think Monty was a worthless varmint like Max and everybody else in Clearwater does."

Jim joined Armstrong beside the small mound of stones.

"I don't think that no more. The way you defended his memory gave me a hint of the man Monty once was. I reckon now that he was a decent man, who caused no harm to anyone, and he just happened to be with my brother when Tyler killed him and his life spiraled downward."

Armstrong nodded and kneeled to pick up another stone.

"It did at that."

Jim placed a hand over his heart. "I, for one, will never speak ill of Monty."

"Then perhaps my work here isn't done." Armstrong placed the stone on the pile and reached for another. "If I can help one man to accept that Monty was decent, I reckon I'll stay until I can persuade another man to come here and pay his respects."

"If you're staying that long, I'll. . . ." Jim bit back the rest of his ill-considered comment, but Armstrong smiled.

"If that was going to be a bad joke, don't worry. Monty had a sense of humor. He'd have laughed." Armstrong removed the smile. He hefted the stone and slammed it down. "Now leave me. I have a friend to bury."

Jim nodded and left Armstrong. He walked down the hill, but halfway down, he veered off to stand in front of a neat and familiar grave.

"Ma, I've arrested the man who I reckon killed our Benny," he said, pointing toward Black Pass. "I hope that'll put Pa out of his torment, but I know you wouldn't want me to condemn an innocent man, so I've got a lot of investigating to do first. Either way, when I've found out the truth, I'll tell you about it. This time, I promise I'll get Pa to come and see you, too."

With that promise made, Jim gave a short nod, swung his hat on his head and strode down the hill to his horse. He'd lost time and, with sundown only a few hours away, he didn't want to risk being late for Luther's threatened return, but he still headed on a wide arc around the outskirts of his father's ranch until he reached Black Pass.

The pass was ten miles to the south of Broken Knee Canyon and was just a short pass on the western route to Green Valley. Jim rode into the pass and pulled his horse to a halt at the point where the sides were at their steepest.

A solitary tree stood there, the strain of being so close to the spot where Benny died probably helping to bow its branches. He dismounted and turned on the spot, examining the rugged sides of the pass.

After so many years he didn't expect to

find anything interesting, but as most people avoided the pass, Jim included, familiarizing himself with this place felt the right thing to do before he resumed his search for Max. There were plenty of places where a man could hide out and fire a fatal shot at someone on the ground.

He thought about scouting around, but instead, mounted his horse and walked it in a short circle, ensuring this deserted place embedded itself on his mind. The thought of just how few people headed through the pass returned to Jim and he turned toward the western end of the pass.

Five miles beyond was Bart Haley's ranch, and this man had ranched here for many years. With his solitary ways, Jim doubted that Hopeman had questioned him. As the sun was dipping below the side of the pass, he shrugged and turned his horse to the pass's western exit.

As he rounded the corner seven riders swung into view. One of the men was Max Malloy, and they were examining the terrain in the same way that Jim had been doing. They turned to him and Jim drew his horse to a halt.

"Max Malloy, I've been looking for you," he shouted.

Without warning, Max drew his gun and fired. The shot flew way over Jim's head, but the other men joined Max in firing. Jim pulled his horse around on the spot and rode away. Gunfire from behind hurried him on his way so he rounded the corner at a gallop.

The moment Max disappeared from view, from ahead, two more riders appeared, riding toward him along the pass. Just as Jim recognized them as being Channing and Grange, they drew their guns and blasted a volley of gunfire that tore through the air around him.

FOUR

Jim flinched as another gunshot whistled by his ear. As the crisp crack of gunfire echoed, he weighed up his prospects of reaching either end of the pass against holing up. Channing blasted a rapid burst of gunfire into the dirt before his horse and resolved his problem for him.

So he turned his horse to the right and headed past the steepest part of the pass and on to a huge rocky outcrop. Under an overhang, he jumped down from his horse and hunkered down behind a boulder that covered him from view from either side of the pass.

He bobbed up as Channing and Grange shuffled down behind a boulder on the other side of the trail, forty yards away and ten yards from the pass bottom. Other movement rippled to their side as at least one other man scurried for cover.

"Ambushing a lawman is a big mistake," Jim shouted. His voice echoed back at him from the other side of the pass.

Jim waited for one of the men to shout back, hoping to gather some clues as to where the remaining men had gone to ground, but they remained silent. On hands and knees he crawled beyond the side of the boulder, but a gunshot ripped into the earth beside his hand, forcing him to scurry back for cover.

"You're facing a heap of trouble for this," he shouted.

Jim crawled to the other side of the boulder, but a gunshot winged into the rock, ripping shards into his face. He reckoned that with the pass sides being so steep, any attempt to climb to safety would expose him for too long.

So, on his belly, Jim snaked to his horse,

the boulder at least giving him cover to get under the overhang without his attackers being able to see him. He stood up. The overhang was only thirty feet wide and, on either side, it had fallen away, leaving no cover between him and his attackers.

As Jim debated mounting his horse and fleeing, on the other side of the pass, the slash of darkness rose as the sun headed for the horizon. Luther had promised to come for Tyler at sundown, and Jim reckoned he was a man who kept his promises.

So even though Max had pinned him down, he had to find a way out. Jim dropped to his knees and crawled toward the covering boulder. Pebbles drizzled to the ground before him. He just had time to realize they'd fallen from the edge of the overhang when another of Max's associates, Lester, dropped from above, landing lightly, but still stumbling to the side.

Jim didn't give Lester time to regain his footing. He rose to his feet and pounded across the ground toward him. On the run, he had time to blast one wild gunshot at Lester. Then he hit him full in the side and knocked him back three paces before both men tumbled to the ground.

Jim's Peacemaker fell from his hand, but he landed on top of his opponent, raised himself high, and then slugged Lester's jaw. Lester shrugged off the blow and bucked him from his chest.

Jim had a firm grip of Lester's arms and the two men rolled to the side, struggling to throw punches at each other from such close quarters. Jim realized that they'd rolled out from the overhang and were now in full view of the men on the other side of the pass.

He clung hold of his opponent, not giving them a clear shot at him. With each man clutching hold of the other's arms as they each tried to wrestle each other down, they rolled one way and then the other, dust pluming up around them.

Gunfire blasted, echoing as it seemingly exploded from more than one position. This surprised Lester as much as it did Jim, and the grip on Jim's arms lessened as Lester tried to find out who had been foolish enough to fire at them when they were so entangled.

Jim took advantage of his opponent's distraction to release his own hold and slug his jaw. Lester's head cracked back but Jim kept hold of him. He rolled over him and grabbed him from behind.

He climbed to his feet and placed Lester's back to him, using him as a human shield. Gunfire rippled again, but this time Jim realized that none of it was directed at him and that it was all coming from farther away.

A lone rider emerged around the long arc of the pass, galloping straight for his position. Jim smiled on recognizing the newcomer as Armstrong. He pulled Lester's gun from its holster and fired up at the opposite side of the pass, aiming for his attackers' position and forcing them to stay down.

With Jim's attention wavering, Lester

used the opportunity to yank his arms free of Jim's grasp and launch a fist backhanded at Jim's chin. Jim raised his arm and deflected the blow with his forearm.

Then he swung his gun up and slugged Lester's temple with the cold metal. Lester rolled with the blow and fell to his knees. He kneeled with his head lolling, and then launched himself to his feet as he ripped a knife from his boot.

Jim darted his head back, saving himself from Lester's wild slash. As Lester thrust his arm forward, aiming to stab him in the belly, Jim fired a low slug that tore into Lester's stomach. Lester still staggered on a half-pace, momentum dragging the knife onward, but Jim fired again, rocking Lester back on his heels before he keeled over on to his back.

Jim turned at the hip and fired two speculative shots at the other side of the pass. Then he collected his own gun from the ground and scurried for his horse. In a lithe action he mounted it and dragged it out from the overhang.

With Armstrong standing square in the middle of the pass and laying down covering fire, he hurried away from the overhang, firing over his shoulder. The echoes made the gunfire sound more intense than just two men could make.

Armstrong fired one last volley. Then he dragged his horse around on the spot, the horse prancing for a moment before he got it under control, and galloped for the western end of the pass.

One of the attackers made the mistake of straying out from his cover and Jim blasted this man through the chest. This encouraged the other men to stay down, so he thrust the gun in his belt and concentrated on putting distance between the attackers and himself, but as he reached the exit, he slowed to let Armstrong draw alongside him.

He confirmed that five men were now in pursuit. They closed: 300 yards, 200, 100, and Armstrong's and Jim's tired horses were slowing with every pace. Jim reloaded both his guns and, when the leading horse was thirty yards behind him, he turned in the saddle and fired.

Armstrong joined him and they laid down an arc of deadly gunfire that ripped into the closest man, knocking him from his horse. His trailing foot caught and let him be dragged along behind his steed.

Gunfire whistled past Jim's head, but he took careful aim at the next nearest man and fired. He wasted three shots, but the fourth grazed the man's shoulder, forcing him to throw up a hand to clutch his wounded shoulder.

A second shot wheeled him to the ground. As Max galloped on to pass the dying man, 200 yards back from him, Channing and Grange galloped out of the pass. Jim holstered his Peacemaker and thrust the other gun into his belt.

With a great roar and a slap of his hand on his horse's rump, he tried to drag a last burst of speed from his steed. At his side, Armstrong did the same and they'd increased the gap to 200 yards by the time he checked behind them.

Jim whooped his delight, but then realized that the increased distance was because Max was slowing. He hoped Armstrong would offer a reason, but he only shrugged. Jim put a hand to his brow.

The men who had come out of the pass had slowed to a halt and were milling in a circle. Max was gesturing to them, urging them to join the chase, but these men were gesturing back and not moving out on to the plains.

Jim didn't wait around to worry about the problems Max was having controlling these men and returned to concentrating on his riding. After another quarter-mile, Max stopped.

Both Jim and Armstrong whooped some more. Then Jim pointed forward at Bart's ranch, some three miles away. Armstrong grunted his agreement and hurried his horse on. The two men rode toward the ranch, and before long Max disappeared into the heat haze behind them.

This encouraged the two men to slow their horses to a trot. With their safety now assured, Jim turned in the saddle to Armstrong.

"I'm much obliged to you for helping me out – again."

"That was no problem for someone who attended Monty's funeral," Armstrong said.

Jim rode on for another minute before he spoke again.

"When you rescued me, you laid down so much gunfire, I thought for a moment I had more than one rescuer."

Armstrong shrugged. "It must have been the echoes."

Jim nodded. "It must have."

With Jim in the lead, they rode on to Bart's land. The rough corral and unkempt wagon showed Bart's lack of interest in any activity beyond earning himself enough to live on. As Bart only ever came into Clearwater to trade and gained no friends with his surly attitude, Jim stopped twenty yards from the front of the small ranch house and waited for him to come out.

Jim was just beginning to think that Bart wasn't here when the grizzled man walked through his door. As Jim had expected, he had a rifle leveled on them.

"That's far enough," Bart said.

Jim raised his hands. "It's Deputy Jim Lawson from Clearwater."

"I don't care who you are." Bart swung to the side to spit on the ground. "You aren't staying on my land."

"I don't aim to stay. I just want to know whether you saw anyone come out of the pass five years ago."

Bart bunched his bristled jaw and then gave a short shrug.

"Five years! You've come here to ask me what I saw five years ago?"

When Jim nodded, with shake of his head, Bart swung the rifle over his shoulder and tipped back his hat. Jim nudged his horse forward to stand in front of Bart. Armstrong stayed back.

"It was after my brother, Benny Lawson, died in the pass. Whoever killed him must have headed west afterward and that meant they'd have gone by your land. I reckon nobody passes here that you don't notice."

"You reckon right." Bart strode out from his house to stand beside Jim's horse and face the pass, his eyes glazing as he appeared to drag up an old memory. "Your father was leading a posse, and I'll tell you what I told him. I saw nothing."

Jim sighed. "Then I'll leave you. I'm obliged for your help."

Jim turned his horse, aiming to join Armstrong, but Bart raised a hand, halting him.

"You didn't listen to what I said." Bart raised his eyebrows and gave a slow wink. "I saw nothing."

"Nothing is nothing."

"It isn't, because like you say, I see everyone that leaves the pass." Bart pointed over Jim's left shoulder. "Just like I can see those riders heading this way."

Jim turned and winced. Max was leading a line of four riders toward the ranch, and they were galloping toward them with their guns brandished.

FIVE

"Are you letting us in your house?" Armstrong said.

Bart faced the approaching riders and then gave a reluctant beckoning wave. So Armstrong and Jim corralled their horses and dashed into the house. Bart stayed in the doorway. Jim urged Bart to follow them in, but Bart shook his head and trained his rifle on the riders.

"Move aside," Max said, drawing his horse to a halt. "We've got business with the deputy."

Bart firmed his rifle against his shoulder and sighted Max.

"You're on my land and unless you want to stay on it permanently, leave now," he said.

Max shared eye-contact with Armstrong and Jim through the windows. He shrugged and tugged on the reins. The flanking men moved to follow him, but Channing and Grange swung their horses around and charged for the house.

Bart blasted at Max, but the man was already leaping from his horse and the lead hurtled over his form. Before Bart could turn around to fire at the other men, simultaneous slugs hammered into his chest from two different directions.

Bart staggered back to crash to the floor. He moved to sit up as Jim dashed to his side to drag him into the house, but another slug ripped into his chest and forced Jim to flinch back.

By the side of the door Jim noted the bullet-ridden body. He shook his head and joined Armstrong at the window. Outside, Max was taking cover behind the water-trough and Channing and Grange had dismounted and were running around the back of the house.

Armstrong hurried the other two men into a hollow with a quick burst of gunfire, and then darted back from the window as Max returned fire. As Armstrong and Max traded shots, Jim confirmed that the door and window at the front were the only way in, and then joined Armstrong in firing through the window.

One man bobbed up, but before he could fire, Armstrong planted a slug in his chest. When Channing and Grange returned and scurried behind Bart's wagon, another man jumped up to cover them, but earned a slug in the neck for his trouble.

After this, Max urged caution and for the next half-hour the men inside and outside traded gunfire. With Max not taking any risks, none of his men gained any positions closer to the house. In a lull, Jim dragged Bart's body farther into the house and then rejoined Armstrong at the window.

"Max, why did you ransack Monty's store?" he shouted.

"I don't have to explain myself to you,"

Max shouted. He rose up to fire at the house, and then ducked. "A snooping lawman like you isn't leaving here alive."

"This is wrong," Armstrong said to Jim. "Monty had nothing worth stealing."

"Perhaps he was looking for something, like he was looking for something in the pass." Jim pointed at Bart's body. "Either way, Max has silenced a potential witness to my brother's murder and, to me, that's mighty suspicious."

Armstrong nodded, fingering his beard. "How did your brother die?"

"I wasn't much involved at the time." Jim shrugged. "I was . . . I was distracted when it happened, but in short, Sheriff Hopeman ran Luther Wade out of town, but his friend, Tyler Coleman, still loitered nearby and he stole a thousand dollars from my father's ranch. A posse headed off after him."

"Was Benny in the posse?"

"Nope. Benny was sixteen and eager to join the chase. My father wouldn't let him, but Benny had the kind of enthusiasm that can make a man great, or will just get him killed."

The two men stood in silence facing the wagon and the water-trough.

"Gene said that Benny would have been a lawman one day."

"He would," Jim said, nodding. "Benny had the instincts, and this was his chance to prove it. He asked around and something Monty said suggested to him that everyone had headed in the wrong direction."

Outside, Max bobbed up from behind the water-trough, but Armstrong blasted a shot over the trough that forced him to duck.

"What hint?"

"I have no idea. Anyhow, he deputized Monty." Jim chuckled. "He had no right to do that, but Benny was the kind of man that naturally gave orders. So they headed off in the opposite direction to the posse, but in Black Pass, the snake ambushed them."

"Tyler Coleman?"

Jim firmed his jaw, but then nodded. "It couldn't have been anyone else. Max followed them, but when he arrived the shooting was all over. Benny had only been shot in the leg, but he'd bled to death. Monty was sitting hunched beside the body and mumbling that he couldn't stop the bleeding. Tyler was long gone, and so was the money."

"If Tyler killed Benny, he must have been vicious to get past Monty."

"That's as maybe, but my father wasn't in no mood for excuses. He searched everywhere, but found no sign of Tyler."

"What happened after the trail went cold?"

"Monty turned to the whiskey, my mother pined away and my father and me have struggled to share a civil word since." Jim blasted a shot at Channing who was daring to edge out from the wagon. "He reckoned there was no point having a lawman for a son if that lawman couldn't catch his brother's killer. He's right."

As Armstrong shrugged, a huge burst of gunfire ripped out from outside, peppering the window and forcing them to duck. When Jim raised his head Grange and Channing were dashing for the door.

He fired at them, but the two men gained a position pressed flat on either side of the door. Grange kicked open the door. Jim swung away from the window and hammered gunfire through the open doorway.

He waited for one of the men to make the mistake of trying to come through the door. Long minutes passed with the door swaying in the breeze. Then Max fired at the window from outside, forcing Armstrong to return fire.

With their forces distracted, Channing scampered through the doorway, running with his head thrust low. Jim fired and the shot whistled over Channing's head. Channing was bent so double that he tumbled himself to the floor and skidded on his shoulder.

While still moving, he fired up. The shot hurtled by Jim's nose and tore into the roof, but this gave Jim enough time to steady his stance and blast down at Channing. His shot thundered into his chest and flattened him, but even as he was firing a second time, Grange charged through the doorway.

Jim jerked to the side to avoid Grange's blast of gunfire, while Armstrong swung from the window and hammered a shot into Grange's back that buckled him almost to his knees. Grange still staggered two paces and fell into the crouched Jim.

From so close he entangled himself in Jim's limbs. Elsewhere in the house more gunfire sounded, but Jim had no choice but to ignore it and concentrate on bundling Grange away from him.

With a mixture of elbows and fists, he knocked Grange to the floor, but Grange, with one last desperate lunge, aimed his gun at Jim, and Jim had no choice but to blast him between the eyes. He turned and beside the door, Armstrong and Max were struggling.

Each clutched the other's wrist as they tried to wrestle Armstrong's gun down to aim it at the other man. Jim rolled to his feet and, with his back to the wall, he faced the two fighting men.

Max accepted he was now outnumbered and swung Armstrong around so that Armstrong stood between him and Jim. With surprising strength, he pulled the gun down inch by inch, turning it inexorably toward Armstrong's head.

He risked one wild shot, the blast close enough to tear Armstrong's hat from his head. Jim edged to the side, but he couldn't get a clear shot at Max.

"Go to the floor," Jim said.

At first Armstrong ignored the plea, but then flinched and released Max's arm. He dropped. Even before he'd hit the floor, Jim had fired two shots into Max's chest that wheeled him around to crash into the wall and slide down it to lie on his front.

From the floor Armstrong nodded his thanks. He hurried around the fallen men in the house, checking they were dead. When he turned Max over he discovered that he was still breathing and gestured for Jim to join him.

Jim hunkered down beside Max and shook his shoulders. Max's eyes rolled before they centered on Jim's face.

"Why?" Jim asked.

"I've got my reasons, but I wasn't after you," Max said, his voice faint and fading with every word. "I was after Monty."

"Are you talking about now or five years ago?"

Max twitched. Pain contorted his face. Then he thrust up a hand to grab Jim's jacket and lever himself up a foot.

"I figured out where Monty was hiding and was all set to stop him talking. Then you arrived." Max's grip loosened and he fell back to lie on the floor. "I guess Luther will just have to. . . ."

Jim shook Max's shoulder, but when his head lolled, he rolled back on his haunches and Armstrong returned an expression that was as bemused as Jim felt.

"I guess he was confused at the end and

couldn't work out the difference between today and five years ago," Armstrong said.

"I guess."

With nothing else to accomplish at the ranch, Armstrong and Jim left the house. As they headed to the corral, Jim pointed at the lengthening shadows, so, in short order, the two men mounted their horses and headed back to Black Pass at a gallop.

Just in case Max had any more help they kept on their guard as they rode through the pass, but no more surprises came and in good time they left the pass and hurried on to Clearwater. By the time the town appeared ahead their horses were straining and they had no choice but to slow to a trot.

"Are you going to tell me who she was?" Armstrong asked.

Jim rode on with his jaw set firm. "She?"

"Yeah," Armstrong said with subdued laughter in his voice. "When Tyler killed your brother, you were too *distracted* to be much involved. To me, that means there was a woman involved."

"I guess there was." Jim sighed. "Her name was Zelma."

Armstrong snorted a deep breath, his eyes flaring for a moment.

"Zelma Hayden?" he said.

"You know her?"

"I know *of* her. Monty once said she was a mighty fine-looking woman."

Jim leaned forward in the saddle, nodding, and then pulled his horse to the side to ride alongside Armstrong.

"She sure was, and we were close. I always assumed we were to wed, but I've had five years to wonder where I went wrong and I can now see that making too many assumptions was my problem. Zelma dreamed of seeing the world; I just wanted to be a lawman in Clearwater. I thought her fancy thoughts would fly away, but one day it was she who flew."

"Did she say why?"

"Nope. I tried to find her. Some people said she met a traveling salesman and went off with him. Some people saw this man, but more people didn't." Jim sighed and slapped his thigh. "So the only thing I knew for sure was that she'd gone and she wasn't coming back."

Armstrong chuckled with companionable laughter and rode on, but as he approached the first buildings on the outskirts of Clearwater he spoke up.

"Did this happen when Benny died?"

"Yeah.

"Do you have any reason to suppose her disappearance had anything to do with his murder?"

"No." Jim narrowed his eyes. "What are you thinking?"

"Nothing." Armstrong turned his horse to ride down the main drag. "I'm just trying to understand what happened."

"Then tell me what you're—"

Gunfire blasted out from Clearwater's main drag. Jim noted the setting sun while Armstrong winced. Then the two men broke into a gallop.

SIX

When Clearwater's main drag swung into view, the situation was as Jim had feared. Strung out across the main drag a line of riders was circling before the sheriff's office, firing high and hollering, ensuring everyone knew they'd arrived.

Luther Wade was in their midst and the rest of the men had the arrogant postures and trigger-happy attitudes of men hired to cause trouble. At the end of the main drag Jim dismounted and, with Armstrong at his heels, hurried for the nearest cover, a row of barrels outside the hardware store.

When he bobbed up, several of Luther's men were taking positions opposite the sheriff's office. Others were taking cover behind sacks, or in the alleyways. The remaining riders flanked the office. Aside from them, the main drag was clearing rapidly as Clearwater's citizens scurried for cover.

"Hopeman, sundown is a-coming and it's time to bring Tyler out," Luther shouted.

"There's no chance of that happening," Hopeman shouted from within the office, making both Jim and Armstrong wince.

"We've got to get into a better position, or we aren't going to help here," Armstrong said.

Jim nodded and pointed as he ordered Armstrong to skirt around the back of town and attack Luther from the other end of the main drag. Armstrong nodded and edged to the wall. Jim joined him and they backed away from Luther, keeping their guns holstered to appear that they weren't aiming to cause trouble.

When they parted, Armstrong ran across the main drag and disappeared behind the church, and Jim dashed around the back of the stables and toward the Rusty Spur. Jim had reached the back of the saloon when a volley of gunfire blasted out on the main drag.

Jim gritted his teeth and charged down the alleyway beside the saloon. At the end, he slid to a halt, but he'd come out level with two men who were hunkered down on the boardwalk and firing at the office.

Jim darted his head back to avoid their seeing him, and when the next volley of gunfire ended, he edged forward again. The nearest man *had* seen him. He fired three rapid shots that whistled past Jim's nose, forcing him to dart back into the alleyway.

Jim debated heading back down the alleyway, but as that'd probably get him a bullet in the back he rocked back on his heels and charged out on to the boardwalk. On the run he ripped an arc of gunfire sideways, scything through the nearest man's chest.

The man staggered off the edge of the boardwalk, his gun falling from his slack fingers as he clutched his chest and rolled to lie sprawled on the ground. The second man turned and blasted lead at Jim.

In desperation, Jim dove to the ground, skidding on his shoulder as he hurtled into the main drag. On the ground, he fired, winging the man's arm and wheeling him away. Jim took more careful aim, but from the saloon roof a man fired down at him, the bullet pluming into the earth beside Jim's arm.

Jim rolled on his back and, with his back braced, fired up. The shot was wild and, with no time to reload, he rolled back to the boardwalk, slugs tearing into the earth behind his tumbling form.

On the boardwalk he rolled to his knees and gathered up the first man's gun. The wounded man was clawing his way down the boardwalk toward him, his gun thrust out, but Jim ripped lead into his chest, slamming him to the wood, and then collected his gun.

He craned his neck out to see the roof, but a warning shot forced him to dart back to the wall. Out on the main drag around a dozen riders circled in front of the sheriff's office, and more men were running in from both sides.

Jim took a deep breath and, with his guns thrust out, charged onto the main drag. He turned on the spot and fired up at the man on the roof. His first shots were wild, but the man clutched his chest and slipped to his knees before he tumbled down the roof.

As he crashed to the ground, Jim found that Armstrong had climbed on to the church roof and, from that vantage point, had shot the man. He acknowledged Jim and then turned and fired down at the riders.

In confusion, they scattered and Jim added to their problems by hunkering down on the edge of the boardwalk and blasting two men from their mounts. Hopeman and Newell, spurred on by this success, flung open the office door and laid down an arc of deadly gunfire that took another two riders.

Luther barked orders and all the men who were on foot fled to their horses, gathering them on the run, and backed them away. Before they could regroup the lawmen and Armstrong peppered gunfire at them from different angles and, in panic, they moved their horses back.

When the lawmen knocked another man from his horse Luther swung his horse around and galloped out of town, throwing up a huge cloud of dust in his desperation to flee Clearwater. His men trailed after him, only a few having the bravado to holler and rip gunfire into the air.

On the run, Jim fired at a straggler who had failed to mount his horse. When both his guns clicked on empty chambers he ran after him and grabbed his arm. The man tried to tear himself away, but Jim gained a firmer grip and pulled him around.

He swung back his fist, ready to slug him to the ground, but then saw the green bandanna around the man's neck, a familiar embroidered pattern covering the corner, and froze. The man cringed, clearly expecting Jim to hit him, but when Jim didn't move, he shook himself free and bundled Jim away.

As Jim floundered on the ground, the man ran to his horse, mounted it and galloped away. Jim rubbed his face, forcing his shock to recede. He reloaded and fired at the fleeing riders, but by then they were all surging out of town.

Still, he dashed to his horse and mounted it. He tugged his steed around and hurried after Luther's men. By the time he passed the sheriff's office, Armstrong had climbed down from the church roof.

He hurried out onto the hardpan to block his way. Jim drew his horse to a halt, almost unseating himself in the process, and moved to pass him, but Armstrong stepped to the side to block his route again.

"Move!" Jim shouted. "They're getting away."

"Let them go, unless you want to die."

The riders were now several hundred yards beyond the edge of town. With a reluctant slap of a fist against his thigh, Jim acknowledged the recklessness of his pursuit and dismounted. As Gene Trentham came out of his workshop to collect his latest business, Jim headed to the sheriff's office.

Armstrong was at his side and his brow was furrowed, but Jim firmed his jaw instead of explaining himself. On the board-walk, Hopeman slapped his back and then moved on to congratulating Armstrong.

The sheriff even offered to deputize Armstrong, but Armstrong refused, although he did accept the offer of a coffee. Inside the office, Jim sat on the edge of his desk as Hopeman walked across the room to stand before the corner cell and face Tyler through the bars. Despite the failure of the rescue attempt, Tyler sat on his cot, clutching his knees to his chest and smiling.

"Don't gloat, Sheriff," he said. "Luther *will* succeed."

Hopeman shook his head and joined Jim, who relayed the details of Max's presumed ransacking of Monty's store in his search for something and then his unsuccessful attempt to ambush him. Throughout, Hopeman snorted his ill-opinion of Max, but when Jim mentioned his idea about Bart Haley being a potential witness, he brightened and then frowned on hearing of his demise.

"That sure is a pity," Hopeman said. "If we're going to convict Tyler, we need proof."

"Bart wanted to tell me something. He thought the fact that he saw nothing was more interesting than I thought it was."

Hopeman nodded. "Perhaps he was right. If the killer didn't leave the pass that way, somebody should have seen him."

Jim bit back mentioning what was obvious to them all. The only man who had come out of Black Pass was Monty.

"Either way, now that Luther has made his intentions clear, it isn't going to be easy to get Tyler to trial," Jim said.

"You're right." Hopeman sighed. "I guess I now have to admit we need help to sort this out."

Hopeman located a scrap of paper on his

desk and scrawled a quick message on it. He passed the note to Deputy Newell and ordered him to go to the telegraph office in Fall Creek as fast as he could and wire a message to Marshal Kirby.

Newell turned to the door, but Jim shuffled off the side of the desk and volunteered to go instead. When Newell raised no objection, Jim took the message from him.

"Come now. Got the man who shot Benny Lawson," Jim said, reading the message. In the doorway, he tipped his hat to Hopeman. "I guess if we're lucky, Kirby will be here by sundown tomorrow."

"I reckon we can sure hold out against Luther for that long," Hopeman said.

SEVEN

Jim rode out of Clearwater. On the edge of town, he slowed and searched for Luther's trail. As he'd half-expected, recent tracks headed toward Broken Knee Canyon, but he wasn't a tracker and, when the canyon appeared on the horizon, the trail had already gone cold.

On his own, he didn't dare head into the canyon, so he spent a fruitless hour scouting around the outskirts of his father's land. He failed to relocate Luther's tracks, so he accepted that he wouldn't be able to both get the message to Marshal Kirby and pick up Luther's trail this evening, so with some reluctance, he headed toward Fall Creek instead.

When he closed on the trail, his father appeared ahead as he used the last of the day's light to patrol his borders. With his hat raised high Jim hailed him. Caleb hailed him back and, despite his need to hurry, Jim stopped.

"Are you fine now, Pa?" he asked when Caleb joined him.

"Yeah." Caleb sighed. "If you're checking up on me to see whether I'm planning to kill Tyler, you don't need to. I've got no desire to see him until he's swinging on the end of a rope."

"I'm glad to hear it, but I'm not checking on you. I'm heading to Fall Creek to get a message to Marshal Kirby."

"To me, you were just roaming around, trying to decide whether or not to see me." Caleb flashed a grim smile. "No matter how bad things are between us, I can't believe you need to do that."

"I *was* roaming around, but I was trying to pick up the tracks of those outlaws who tried to free Tyler. Luther roared into town and fair shot up the place, but we saw him off."

"You did well, but you were looking in the

wrong place. Aside from you, nobody's passed by me all day."

"I'm obliged for the information." Jim turned to the trail, but Caleb raised a hand and he turned back.

"Are you worried this Luther might try to seize Tyler again?"

"If I don't get help from Marshal Kirby, he might."

Caleb nodded. He hunched his shoulders and, for just a moment, his eyes flashed with a hint of warmth. When he spoke, his carefree voice suggested the considerate man who had enlightened Jim's childhood years.

"Son, let me pass that message on for you, and you can carry on searching for him." Caleb smiled, but when Jim shook his head, he removed his hat and clutched it before him. "It'll be my way of apologizing for nearly shooting Tyler, and for just accusing you and for everything I've . . . everything."

Unable to face encouraging a discussion that he didn't think he'd ever have, but to which he now didn't have the time to devote, Jim regarded the many places in which Luther's gang could have holed up and then noted the red glow on the western horizon. He nodded and passed Caleb the note Hopeman had given him.

"Maybe once this is over we can. . . ." Jim coughed to clear his throat, finding that he couldn't even ask whether he could visit the family home for the first time since his mother had died.

"Maybe."

Caleb pocketed the note and, without further word, swung his horse around to head toward Fall Creek, leaving Jim to turn to the hills. He took his father's advice and resumed his search out of sight of his father's land, but, as the light-level plummeted, he still couldn't find Luther's tracks, so he decided to use the weak rays of the low crescent moon to risk scouting into the first length of the canyon.

He did resolve to stay within a few minutes' riding of the entrance. The barren gash that was the canyon was twenty miles long and consisted of one long arc with only the most withered of vegetation flanking its rocky sides.

On either side of the trail, a tangle of caves, boulders and weathered rock formation spread out. So when Jim reached the canyon, he hunched forward in the saddle and examined each passing cave and source of a likely ambush while maintaining a brisk pace.

He found tracks, but nothing to confirm that Luther had headed here, so within fifteen minutes, he turned to leave, but as he reached the exit, a lone rider was standing on the trail, facing him. Jim smiled and hailed the rider.

"What are you doing here, Armstrong?" he said.

"Hopeman ordered me to scout around while you sent that message." Armstrong raised his eyebrows with a silent question and when Jim just drew alongside, he pointed at the ground. "I reckon we're both interested in these."

Jim examined the messed-up ground, seeing nothing but the prints he'd found earlier, their forms almost lost in the shadows.

"What am I looking at?"

"The prints made by a group of riders as they hurried into the canyon." Armstrong smiled. "I reckon they'll be Luther's tracks."

Jim kept his jaw firm. "What makes you think I'm looking for him?"

"Because I reckon you've got someone else to deliver that message, and searching for Luther's gang is the only thing I can think of that you could be doing. The trouble is, I don't know why you're doing it – unless you've got yourself a death wish."

Jim shrugged. "You're right about what I'm doing, but I've got no intention of explaining myself."

"I thought as much." Armstrong turned to the darkening interior of Broken Knee Canyon and then turned back to Jim. "Still, do you want some help in finding him?"

* * *

Luther's encampment was in a narrow gully and set back from the main trail through the canyon. His gang had slipped under an overhang that hid them from view from all directions but head on.

Their campfire was low and guarded and just strong enough to drive away the night chill. Their horses were tethered in the deepest part of the overhang. In the thirty minutes since Armstrong and Jim had reached the edge of the slope opposite, they had showed no inclination to take their horses to the dribbling stream that ran through the gully.

Now, with the full onset of night, the men bustled around the campfire, passing plates around. With the men now confident in their security, their voices grew louder and boisterous. When they'd eaten, they nomin-ated Woodward – Jim learned his name from the taunts they directed at him – to water their horses on the basis that he was the last one to leave Clearwater earlier.

On his own, Woodward led the horses down to the stream. As he passed their position, Jim leaned over the edge of the slope. With his eyes narrowed, he confirmed that he *was* the man with the green bandanna. When Jim shuffled back, Armstrong leaned toward him.

"Are we going to ambush them?" he asked. "Or are we just going to watch them?"

"You're going to watch them. I'm going to ambush this one."

Before Armstrong could question his orders, Jim patted Armstrong's shoulder and slipped back from the edge. Bent double he scurried from his position and down the slope, keeping about thirty yards back from Woodward and staying in the deep shadows between the boulders that flanked the gully.

When he emerged by the stream, Woodward was around thirty yards to his right and facing the horses. Jim confirmed that he wasn't being particularly observant, and slipped around the edge of a tangle of undergrowth until he was ten yards back from him. He stood tall and drew his Peacemaker, not risking alerting him by trying to get closer.

"Reach," he ordered.

Woodward flinched and turned at the hip, his hand whirling to his gun, but the gun aimed at his chest made him raise his hand.

"What do you want with me?" he said and narrowed his eyes. "Deputy."

Jim judged that they were some distance from the campsite so unless Woodward shouted he was unlikely to attract anyone's attention. He ordered Woodward to drop his gunbelt, and then pointed at the bandanna around his neck.

"Where did you get that?"

Woodward raised a hand to finger the bandanna, displaying the embroidered letter Z in the corner, and shrugged. He blinked, and when he spoke his voice was lower and less assured than before.

"I've had it a long time."

"There was a woman who lived in

Clearwater five years ago when Tyler Coleman was here, but she disappeared."

"I've got no idea what you—"

"You *do* know something." Jim firmed his gun hand. "You'll tell me why you're wearing the bandanna I gave Zelma Hayden."

Woodward shuffled from foot to foot, but he glanced over Jim's right shoulder. Jim stood tall, listening. Then, on hearing a crunch as of a foot grinding into loose dirt, he turned at the hip and arced his Peacemaker around.

When he was fully turned it was to face Luther, his other men spread out around him with their guns aimed at him. In their midst was Armstrong with two men holding him from behind with his arms thrust up his back. To Luther's grunted command, Jim threw his gun on the ground, but he still stood with his posture casual and ready to make a stand if the chance presented itself.

"What are you doing with Woodward?" Luther asked, pacing forward from the group to stand in front of Jim.

"I'm asking him a question. He'll answer it either here or in jail, but I will get an answer."

Luther snorted and folded his arms. "About what?"

"It's the woman," Woodward said. "He's asking about the woman."

Armstrong grunted and tried to wrestle himself free of the men holding him, but they gripped his arms more tightly. Still he struggled and, with a huge lunge of his right arm, hurled one of the men from him.

Using the distraction, Jim dropped to one knee, his questing hand lunging for his gun, but a warning shot from Luther plumed into the ground, inches from his fingers, and forced him to raise his hand and stand up. With at least ten men training their guns on him, he couldn't aid Armstrong's attempted escape.

Armstrong scrambled himself free of the other man holding him, but by then, Luther was at his side. At the moment Armstrong gained his freedom, Luther swung his gun backhanded, clipping Armstrong's temple.

The blow landed with a dull thud, spinning Armstrong away and, in an instant, he slumped to the ground. Luther tapped a foot against his chest. When Armstrong didn't even return a grunt, he turned to Woodward.

"How did he learn about the woman?" he said.

Woodward slipped the bandanna from his neck and waved it at Luther.

"He recognized this."

"That's mighty interesting." Luther stalked past Woodward to Jim's side.

"I want an answer from one of you," Jim said and jutted his jaw. "Why do you have it?"

Luther licked his thin lips and rubbed his chin with the barrel of his gun.

"Have you got some kind of feelings for her?"

"I did, but that was many years ago." Jim gulped. "Now I just want to know what you did with her, whatever that may be."

Luther holstered his gun and backed away from Jim. He paraded before him, throwing out his legs with exaggerated movements. On the fifth pass, he stopped and smiled.

"That truth will cost." Luther gave a low chuckle. "I'll tell you what happened to Zelma when Tyler goes free."

"Tyler isn't going free."

"Then you'll remain ignorant." Luther walked back and forth before Jim twice more, but then swung to a halt and cocked his head to the side. "You'll die in ignorance on this very spot."

"Why you—" Jim raised a fist and advanced on Luther, but Woodward grasped his arm from behind and held him back. Jim stood with his arm raised, and then rolled his shoulders and threw Woodward away from him to stand free. "You won't get away with this."

"I will." Luther drew his gun and sighted Jim's forehead. "If you want to hear the truth about Zelma, you will deliver Tyler to me, or die."

EIGHT

"I'm a lawman," Jim said. "There's no way I'm breaking the law for you."

Luther tightened his trigger finger. His eyes widened.

"Then you'll—"

A gunshot ripped out. Despite his determined stance, Jim flinched and staggered back a pace when the gun wheeled from Luther's hand. Luther turned his head to search for who had shot at him and then leaped for his gun, but a second shot blasted it away from his questing fingers.

He barked out an order and his men dropped to their haunches. They took up defensive positions and blasted in all directions, firing blindly into the darkness.

One man spun back as a high slug ripped into his neck and a second man toppled forward as lead scythed into his stomach.

Luther urged everyone to fall back. He lunged for Jim, but Jim took advantage of everyone's confusion. He batted Luther's hand away and slugged his jaw, the blow wheeling him to the ground.

With his head down, he ran for Luther's gun. He dove, rolling over the gun and dragging it into his grasp. He continued the roll until he came up on his feet and running for the men guarding Armstrong.

Both these men were trying to drag their prisoner into the lee of a giant boulder, but Jim hammered lead into the first man, slamming him back against the boulder. A second shot from his hidden rescuer cut the second man's legs from under him.

Sustained gunfire erupted around Jim, and it was all wild firing from the outlaws and aimed in no particular direction. He slid to a halt beside Armstrong and took his arm. Armstrong's eyes were rolling, so Jim slapped his face.

"We've got one chance to escape," he said. "Either move or die."

Armstrong gave a determined nod and pushed himself to his feet. He stood stooped and swaying, but then turned and, with Jim thrusting a hand under his arm, they shuffled into the darkness.

Luther barked out orders to recapture them, so Jim shuffled into the undergrowth, seeking the darkest shadows. Within seconds of brushing past the first tangle of coarse twigs, footsteps pounded after him.

Lead whistled past his shoulder and Jim turned at the hip. A man was running after him, so Jim blasted this man in the chest, the man so close he ran on for a few paces before barging into him.

Jim shrugged him off and stood for a moment, waiting for the next attacker, but when nobody followed him, he turned. With Armstrong growing in strength with every pace, they moved ever farther into the darkness, heading for the densest patch of undergrowth they could find. Luther continued to shout orders, but they grew fainter and he was getting no discipline from men who were pinned down by determined gunfire.

"Do you have any idea who our mystery savior is?" Armstrong asked when they paused for breath.

"I haven't." Jim released his hold of Armstrong's arm and let him sit down. Then he hunkered down in a guarding position. "But we need to be quiet."

"And grateful," Armstrong said.

* * *

It was well into the night when Jim and Armstrong returned to Clearwater. Their rescuer's gunfire had forced Luther to scurry back to his camp, and they had taken that opportunity to return to their horses and leave Broken Knee Canyon.

They found no hint as to who had rescued them, not that they stayed long enough to search for any clues. When they returned to Clearwater, Jim didn't want to explain why he'd gotten them into such a dangerous situation, so he said nothing beyond confirming that the message to Marshal Kirby had been wired.

While he'd been away Deputy Newell had searched Max Malloy's house and found nearly $1,000 in small bills. This suggested that Max had been involved with Tyler in the robbery that led to Benny's death five years ago, but like everything else Jim had learned recently, that raised more questions than it provided answers.

That night, Hopeman left Jim and Newell on duty while he rode out of town to sleep in a secure spot just off the eastward trail. Armstrong covered the westward trail. With the main routes into Clearwater guarded, Hopeman reckoned the chances of Luther arriving unexpectedly were low.

Even so, Newell and Jim alternated between guarding and sleeping. With Newell taking the first opportunity to sleep, Jim paced around the office, his thoughts whirling with the discovery that Luther's outlaws knew something about Zelma's disappearance. He stood in front of the cell and, for the first time, faced the prisoner through the bars.

"I hope you aren't getting too settled," he said. "Marshal Kirby will be taking you to trial before long and then. . . ." Jim slipped a finger beneath his collar and raised his chin, displaying his neck to Tyler, and gulped.

"We both know I won't swing." Tyler sneered. "You have no proof, and either way, Luther will get me out of here."

"He won't. Your friend had more than twenty men, but we ran him off."

"That was just a testing sortie." Tyler smirked, his eyes bright with arrogance. "Save yourself the trouble. Let me go now."

Jim wondered whether he should question him, and so perhaps learn something that would help his investigation, or perhaps even offer clues as to what had happened to Zelma. As he didn't want to give the man who had shot his brother and destroyed his family an opportunity to gloat, he headed to his desk.

Behind him, Tyler chuckled and rolled on to his cot. Jim still sat down and contented himself with listening to the bustle outside diminish as the evening wore on. Around midnight Jim woke Newell.

While Newell guarded the door Jim carried out the night's first patrol. He strode in a square outside, heading to the four corners where stood the store, the bank, the stables and the saloon.

When he returned he reported the absence of people outside. As Newell locked the door, he sat at his desk. He pulled his hat over his face, rocked his feet on to his desk and shuffled down in his chair.

His problems still reverberated in his mind, but the day had been long and tiring and within minutes lethargy crept into his limbs. Just as the first hints of sleep were dragging him under, a creak sounded nearby.

Jim raised his hat while Newell was already standing by the door, his ear cocked high. Then it came again – a creak, as of someone creeping across the roof. Purely using their eyes, Jim and Newell debated whether they should investigate.

They decided that Newell should, and the deputy slipped outside, after which Jim edged the door closed behind him and stood by it. For long moments Jim waited for Newell to return, but when five minutes had passed he tiptoed into the doorway and hissed an urgent and low request outside.

Again he waited, but the night was as silent as it had been when he had patrolled and the creak from above didn't return, so he hissed another request to Newell. Still no response came, so this time he walked out on to the boardwalk, his Peacemaker raised and pressed flat to his cheek, his ears straining for the slightest noise.

A creak sounded behind him and Jim turned around, his gun arcing toward whoever had produced the noise, but a heavy weight thudded into the side of his head and he dropped to his knees. Heavy footfalls pounded by him, but his vision was blurred and darkness dragged him down.

Darts of light and disorientating visions of the boardwalk outside the office swam around Jim. When he eventually clawed his way back to consciousness he was sure that he had been unconscious for only a few minutes.

He sat up, rubbing the side of his head, feeling a hard lump above his ear, but guessing that his sudden movement had stopped the man from clubbing him across the temple and possibly knocking him out for longer. Farther down the boardwalk lay Newell, his top half on the boardwalk, his feet on the hardpan.

Jim crawled toward him, but when he saw the open office door he slowed to a halt. He stood up, swayed and staggered to the office. With a shaking hand, he held on to the doorframe. Then, with his Peacemaker thrust out before him, he swung into the office.

The room was deserted and the corner cell door was open and swinging. Tyler Coleman had gone.

NINE

Jim lowered his head, taking deep breaths to regain his composure, and then hurried outside. The main drag was still and there was no sign of where the kidnapper had taken Tyler. Still groggy, he hunkered down beside the comatose Newell and slapped his face.

He couldn't rouse him, so he dashed to his horse. He raised a foot to mount his steed, but then lowered it. He had intended to hurry out of town and alert Sheriff Hopeman, but for a reason he couldn't fathom, he was reluctant to do that.

Jim reckoned he had only been unconscious for a few minutes, yet the kidnapper had melted into nowhere. Sneaking into town quietly and freeing Tyler didn't seem like Luther's tactics.

Knocking out himself and Newell didn't seem the sort of activity Luther would do either. Riding into town, hollering his arrival and firing in all directions seemed to be Luther's approach.

That suggested the kidnapper wasn't following Luther's orders, and that maybe he hadn't left town either. So Jim walked out onto the hardpan, searching for likely hiding-places.

The door to Monty's store was open. That wasn't unusual – after Max had ransacked the place there was nothing to steal and Armstrong had been using it as his base, but when he'd completed his patrol earlier the door had been closed.

He headed to the store. On the boardwalk, he raised his Peacemaker and entered the building. His eyes were already accustomed to the gloom and within moments he picked out the hunched form in the far corner of the store.

He narrowed his eyes as he walked toward it and, after two more paces, resolved the form as being the bound and gagged Tyler. In the corner, Tyler's eyes were small embers in the dark.

With his Peacemaker held beside his cheek, Jim crossed the room, walking sideways until he reached Tyler. As he reached out to remove Tyler's gag, a firm footfall sounded behind him.

"Stop right there," a voice said.

Jim flinched, but on recognizing Armstrong's voice, he withdrew his hand and stood tall.

"It's me, Jim."

"I know, but if you don't leave Tyler you'll make me do something I don't want to do," Armstrong said, his tone harsh.

Jim walked around on the spot to confront Armstrong, who stood before the door, the light from outside framing his bulky form. Armstrong's gun was held low with the barrel aimed at his stomach and glinting in a stray beam of light, but Jim kept his hands high and his voice light.

"We both know you won't hurt me."

With a shrug Armstrong holstered his gun. "You're right, but damn it, Jim, I'm just doing what you've thought about doing for the last few hours. So just walk away and let me help you."

Jim cocked his head to the side. "I can't do that. I'm a lawman and I won't break the law to . . . to get information. So stand aside and let me return Tyler to his cell."

Armstrong beckoned for Jim to join him. Jim sighed and then followed Armstrong out on to the boardwalk.

"You need to know about Zelma Hayden," Armstrong said. "So does it matter what happens to Tyler?"

"I'm desperate to know about her, but I can't release the man who I reckon killed my brother. Only the court can decide his guilt, and releasing Tyler sure won't provide justice for my family."

Armstrong snorted. He shook his head and then fingered his beard.

"I thought you knew. Luther doesn't want you to free Tyler because he's his friend. He wants you to release him so he can kill him."

Jim narrowed his eyes. "How do you figure that out?"

"Because Tyler wouldn't ride into Clearwater and almost certain arrest unless he had a mighty good reason. As he reckons the court will clear him, you're protecting him while Luther gets himself so riled he'll get himself killed."

Jim shook his head. "Whether I believe that or not, I can't release a man who is in my custody."

Jim moved to return to the store, but Armstrong grabbed his arm, halting him.

"You know Judge Plummer will find Tyler innocent. That'll destroy your father. Letting Luther kill Tyler will at least give him a chance to move on."

"I'm a lawman. I won't decide a man's guilt." Jim shrugged away from Armstrong and turned to the door. "But I'll find a way to get justice for my brother and discover what happened to Zelma without doing Luther's bidding."

* * *

Jim locked Tyler up and then dragged Deputy Newell into the office and roused him. When Newell was sufficiently alert, Jim told him what he hoped would be a plausible version of events.

He had come out of the office, found Newell unconscious, searched and then found a lone, would-be kidnapper attempting to leave town with Tyler. He had wrested Tyler from him, but the man had escaped.

When he'd finished his explanation, Tyler didn't contradict him, and Newell headed out of town to report what had happened to Hopeman, who returned to hear the report first hand. Jim hated lying, but he ran through his story, keeping the details – and the lies – to a minimum.

As Hopeman believed the tale and saw no reason to change their tactics, they returned to their previous routine of Hopeman and Armstrong guarding the routes into Clearwater and Jim and Newell taking turns to sleep. The rest of the night passed without incident and, at sunup, Hopeman and Armstrong returned to the office.

With nobody in the mood for conversation, the four men set in for a quiet day of waiting for Marshal Kirby. An hour into the day, a messenger arrived and reported that the marshal and a group of deputies had boarded the train in Green Valley and they would be in Fall Creek by early afternoon.

With this good news the lawmen tucked into breakfast, their mood lightening. Two hours later another messenger arrived to report that a dozen or more rough types had descended on the telegraph office in Fall Creek.

Despite the efforts of the office to confuse them, they'd discovered the message that Marshal Kirby was on his way. Then they'd left, heading west along the train tracks toward the approaching train. Hopeman pressed for more details, but although the messenger was only passing on the inform-ation second hand, everything pointed to this gang being Luther Wade's men.

"Marshal Kirby will see them off," Hopeman said. "I've never met that lawman, but everyone says he's formidable."

"Even Kirby could struggle against that many men," Jim said, "but I could intercept the train and escort him on a safe route here."

Hopeman rubbed his chin as he consid-ered, and then nodded.

"I'll go with him," Armstrong said, jumping to his feet.

Jim opened his mouth to complain, but Hopeman's firm-jawed expression said he supported Armstrong's offer, so he nodded and turned to the door. With Armstrong beside him they left the office and without debate rode out of town.

Fall Creek was three hours away and on the way neither man discussed what had happened last night. Although, from

Armstrong's clenched jaw, Jim gathered what he thought of his refusal to let him release Tyler.

With both men being lost in their own thoughts, they didn't waste time and arrived at a water-tower fifty miles down the tracks from Fall Creek in good time. With a few terse comments they agreed to await the train here.

For twenty minutes they stood on either side of the tracks. Jim faced west toward the oncoming train and Armstrong faced east in case Luther was still heading down the tracks. Now the silence preyed on Jim's thoughts and he backed down the track to stand beside Armstrong.

"I guess I'm obliged to you for volunteering for this," he said.

"Somebody had to stop you getting yourself killed," Armstrong said, his jaw set firm. "I don't understand why you wanted to come here. I'm sure that marshal can take care of himself."

"Every source of information has turned

up blank, and I reckon Luther is my last chance of getting proof that Tyler killed my brother." Jim sighed. "If I get the chance to capture him, can I trust you?"

"You can," Armstrong said, his tone hurt. "I'd do nothing to endanger the life of a lawman."

Jim nodded. "But you would try to free the man who killed my brother."

"I told you my reasoning. I was just helping you by doing something you couldn't do yourself." Armstrong turned to Jim. "You can trust me."

"Then I will," Jim said, and made to head back down the track.

"You never explained your full reasoning," Armstrong snapped, his harsh tone halting Jim. "I'd like to know whether I can trust you when the bullets start flying."

"I guess I deserve that." Jim sighed. "I can't say it clearer than the fact that I'm a lawman. I have to do the right thing."

"Even if that means never knowing what happened to a woman you once loved?"

"Yeah. Knowing her fate won't bring her back."

"She doesn't have to be dead. You could be risking her life by not letting Luther have Tyler."

This comment dragged a rumble from Jim's guts. From the moment he'd seen the bandanna he'd assumed the outlaws had killed Zelma.

"Even that," Jim said. He raised his jaw and firmed his voice. "Yeah, even that. It isn't my place to make the rules. I just—"

"Don't lecture me on what is right and what is wrong. I just know that no law is in the right if it might hurt an innocent woman just because of a worthless man like Tyler."

Jim flared his eyes. "Then I can't explain my reasoning to you."

Jim bunched the reins and with a determined swing of his arms he turned his horse and headed down the track.

"You can't, but answer me this," Armstrong shouted after him. "If you're so sure of your actions, why didn't you tell

Sheriff Hopeman about Zelma? Why didn't you tell him what I tried to do last night?"

Jim slowed his horse to a halt and as he turned to Armstrong, the train appeared ahead, its shimmering form emerging from out of the low heat haze.

"The train's a-coming," he said.

Armstrong uttered a low snort and nudged his horse forward to join Jim.

"Are you avoiding answering because you don't know, or because you dare not admit the answer to yourself?"

"Does it matter?"

"Yeah, because I might get another chance to resolve your problem, and knowing what you really want will help me decide what I should do."

"Then remember this," Jim said, waggling a finger at Armstrong. "I won't break the law and I won't let you break the law either."

"Then I understand you."

Jim nodded. "What about you? Because I still don't understand why you risked your own life with that misguided plan to help me."

Armstrong nodded ahead. "The train's a-coming."

Jim waited, but when no further answers were forthcoming, he turned to the train.

TEN

When the train arrived Jim and Armstrong boarded it while the engineers took on water. From the engineers' brisk attitude and the passengers' calm demeanor, Jim reckoned they hadn't seen Luther. So after securing their horses in the end car, they walked down through the cars, searching for Marshal Kirby.

"Have you got any idea what this marshal looks like?" Armstrong asked when they reached the last car.

"Nope, but his sort are usually obvious." Jim smiled and nodded toward the end of the car. "I reckon that's our man."

A group of men had commandeered the end of the car. They sprawled over the seats and their surly silence had forced the middle of the car to remain unoccupied. In their midst sat a man in a black coat, his gray-flecked and trim mustache nestling beneath an aquiline nose and flint eyes.

Jim reckoned he was watching their reflections in the window. Jim took the lead in filing down the aisle. As he entered the unoccupied part of the car the men turned to him. One man thrust out a leg across the aisle, blocking Jim's route.

"Where are you going?" the man asked.

"I'm here to meet the marshal," Jim said. He put on a huge and false smile. "I'd be obliged if you'd let us join you."

"Join us?" The man snorted. "We've got no use for no new deputies."

Outside, the conductor's hollering rippled down the car and with a lurch the train started off for Fall Creek. Jim rested a hand on a seat to keep his balance.

"We don't want to be deputy marshals. I'm Sheriff Hopeman's deputy." Jim gestured over his shoulder. "This here is—"

"You didn't listen. We've got no need for *anyone* joining us."

"I'd prefer to hear that from the marshal."

As the man sneered, the man Jim presumed was Marshal Kirby turned to Jim.

"Why are you still here?" he said, his voice low and uninterested.

"I'm escorting you to Clearwater."

Kirby feigned a yawn. "I know the way."

"I'm sure you do, but you don't know that Luther Wade's gang intercepted your message saying you were coming. They'll be lying in wait somewhere between here and Clearwater."

"And?"

"And I know plenty of hidden trails. I reckon we should get off the train before Fall Creek and use them."

"Do you?" Kirby snorted, his comment dragging a barked laugh from the other men. "I don't need no deputy sheriff from some no-hope town like Clearwater ordering me around."

"That isn't an order. It was a suggestion."

Kirby sneered. "I'll tell you what you can do with your suggestion."

Kirby leaned forward and offered Jim a physically impossible set of activities he could do to himself on his way back to Clearwater. Throughout, Jim remained stone-faced and when the tirade ended, he raised his eyebrows.

"If I tried to do that, my saddle would get in the way, but either way, the suggestion is sound."

Kirby turned aside. "Either way, stay out of my way."

"We aren't." Jim pointed to the nearest unoccupied seat. "We're with you all the way to Clearwater and, if necessary, all the way back to Green Valley."

Kirby muttered another taunt, but Jim didn't stay to hear it and headed to his seat. Armstrong lingered for a moment and then sat down beside Jim. As the train built up to its full speed, he leaned toward Jim.

"He can't treat you like that," he said.

Jim shrugged. "Kirby is no different to

most U.S. marshals I've met. They're all as arrogant as they come, until you prove your worth."

"Do you reckon before we reach Clearwater we'll get the chance to prove our worth?"

Jim nodded. He folded his arms and leaned back in his seat. The landscape passed by as he searched for any sign that Luther was attempting to raid the train, but for the next hour the train trundled along without incident.

Fifteen miles out of Fall Creek the train pulled into Lockwood, the last stop before their destination. Along the platform, the only people waiting for the train were two elderly women. Marshal Kirby was leaning back in his chair with his hat pulled over his eyes, and his deputies were maintaining their studied bored attitude.

"They just don't seem interested," Armstrong said.

"That's what they want everyone to think, but one of them will have already checked who got on board," Jim said.

Within two minutes, the train lurched to a start. Jim was just settling down into his seat again when two men dashed from the station house and headed for the train. They chased along the platform to gain the same speed as the train.

With a helping hand from the conductor, they jumped on board as the train trundled out of the station. Jim patted Armstrong's shoulder, but Armstrong was already leaning to the side as these men disappeared from view.

"The first man was Woodward," he said. "The other man was Jameson, one of the men that jumped me in Broken Knee Canyon."

Jim patted his holster. "Then an ambush is imminent."

Armstrong swung from his seat and moved to head down the car toward Kirby, but Jim took his arm and drew him back. With a single raised eyebrow, he conveyed that this was their chance to prove their worth.

Armstrong rocked back and forth on his heels, but then nodded. With that agreement they headed down the car. Jim kept his head set forward and left the car. One at a time, he and Armstrong jumped over the gap to the second car and slipped inside.

With Jim leading they walked down the car, both men checking out each passenger as they searched for Woodward and Jameson, but they reached the end without seeing them. They were shrugging when the door opened to reveal Woodward standing in the doorway.

Woodward flinched and slammed the door shut. Jim broke into a run and reached the door a few seconds after it closed. He stood by the wall as he waited for Armstrong to join him, and then threw open the door.

As Woodward wasn't there, he dashed through the doorway and headed for the door to the next car. When he opened that door, Woodward still wasn't visible. Both men raised their heads to the train roof and then exchanged a nod.

Jim climbed up the ladder on the side of the car. He raised himself, but a gunshot scythed past his ear and into the wall behind him, forcing him to duck. He counted to ten and rose up again.

Woodward and Jameson were shuffling down the roof and away from him. Keeping his body pressed flat to the side of the train, Jim snaked up the last two steps and rolled on to the roof.

He lay flat and waited for Armstrong to join him. Then the two men edged down the roof after Woodward and Jameson. They stayed doubled over with their hands held out to help them maintain a steady path despite the swaying of the train.

Woodward checked behind him. He grunted and attracted Jameson's attention. The two men turned and hunkered down. They blasted a single shot apiece at them, but the train was swaying so much the shots were wild.

Even so, Jim and Armstrong hurled

themselves flat and, with their elbows braced against the roof, they took careful aim at the two men. In return, Woodward and Jameson ripped out four shots at them.

Two slugs whistled over their heads and two cannoned into the roof before them. Jim and Armstrong attuned themselves to the rhythm of the train and fired. Jim's shot was wild, while Armstrong's tore into Jameson's shoulder, spinning him around and to his knees.

Woodward fired again. Then he turned and took hold of Jameson's unhurt arm. With Woodward holding Jameson up, the two men lumbered down the roof away from them and, after a short run, vaulted the gap to the next car and headed on.

Jim fired another speculative shot and rolled to his feet. With Armstrong at his side, they ran down the roof. They reached the gap, vaulted it and charged after the fleeing men, gaining on them with every pace.

Woodward turned his head and flinched,

possibly in surprise at finding how \
they were. He fired over his shoulder, ⲟ̣ᴇ
bullet scything past Jim's arm and, as
Woodward took more careful aim, Jim
threw himself down to slide across the roof
and plow into Woodward's legs.

Woodward tumbled over Jim's sliding
form. Jim was the first to right himself. He
turned and, on his back, fired sideways at
Woodward. From close range, the shot tore
into Woodward's stomach.

A pained screech escaped Woodward's
lips. He staggered toward Jim on his knees,
his hands clutching at his belly. With his
eyes rolling, he fell on him, his body pressing Jim's gun hand into the roof.

Armstrong and Jameson were now
slugging it out. Jameson was injured, but he
kept his bloodied shoulder away from
Armstrong and led with his right fist. After
delivering two wild round-armed blows that
whistled short of Armstrong's head,
Armstrong moved in with both his hands
clutched together, aiming to hammer

Jameson from the roof.

With surprising grace, Jameson ducked the blow and, as Armstrong teetered, off-balance, he kicked Armstrong's legs from under him. Armstrong landed heavily on his back and, as he floundered, Jameson scrambled for his gun and aimed it down at Armstrong's chest.

Five feet to his side, Jim squeezed his arm out from beneath Woodward and ripped a low shot into Jameson's hip. Jameson staggered a pace, his gun falling from his slackening fingers. A second shot to the back wheeled him from the roof.

As Armstrong nodded his thanks, Jim grabbed Woodward's arm to tug him away, but Woodward's head rose and, with a short head-butt, he slammed his forehead into Jim's nose. The blow came from close to and was weak, but it surprised Jim and snapped his head back to slam into the roof.

He shook himself and, through blurred vision, saw Woodward aim his gun at him. Jim raised his own gun, but a shot rang out.

Jim gritted his teeth, but Woodward rocked back on his haunches and tumbled away, gunsmoke rising from a hole in his back.

As he fell his clawed lunge grabbed Jim's jacket and his weight dragged Jim with him. The two men rolled to the side of the roof. In desperation, Jim dug his elbows in, but he couldn't get enough traction and slid to the edge of the roof.

Woodward plummeted over the side, his body disappearing from sight, and in a moment, Jim was following him, Woodward's death grip dragging him down. At speed, he slid over the edge, but scrambling sounded from behind and Armstrong's hands clutched his waist, stopping his flight with a jarring shudder.

When he'd blinked away his shock, it was to find that Woodward had a firm grip of his arm and was dangling below him. Jim was bent over the edge at the waist, and Armstrong was holding him.

"It seems we'll both die," Woodward said with mocking laughter in his voice.

"Nobody has to die," Jim said.

Woodward threw up his left arm and grasped Jim's right arm, grunting with the effort. The extra grip dragged Jim another few inches forward toward the ground that sped past below him.

"You'll regret shooting me." Woodward chuckled. "It'll be a painful end for you lying by the track with a whole lot of broken bones."

"Even with those bullets in you, you could still live. Quit struggling and I'll get you to a doctor."

"And then?"

"That depends on what you've done, especially about what you did with Zelma."

"I'm telling you nothing about. . . ." Woodward grimaced, his eyes glazing as his grip weakened. He slid down Jim's arm. "I'm . . . I'm. . . ."

His hand opened and he slipped from Jim, so Jim lunged and grabbed Woodward's wrist. He held on, but Woodward dangled slackly in his grip, swaying with his bandanna whipping behind him.

"Tell me about her!" Jim shouted.

"I can't," Woodward said, his voice fading and his eyes darkening. He flashed a weak, sneering smile. "Only Tyler knows."

ELEVEN

Woodward's head lolled. Jim shook him, but the man just rocked from side to side beneath him. When he felt his own body slip another few inches down the side of the train, he had no choice but to release Woodward's body.

First he lunged with his left hand and swiped the bandanna from Woodward's neck. Then he let Armstrong drag him back on to the roof.

"Only Tyler knows," Armstrong intoned. "Just what have they done to her?"

"I've got no idea." Jim fingered the bandanna, but to suppress the memories of the day he'd given this present to Zelma he slipped it into his pocket. "I guess I can't worry about that now. That ambush must be imminent."

As the station at Fall Creek was a half-mile ahead, Armstrong nodded. With no more discussion they climbed down from the roof and returned to the end car. The noise they'd raised and the bodies falling from the roof had attracted the attention of the passengers, and they shied away as Jim and Armstrong headed back to their car.

Jim wasn't in the mood for providing explanations and he walked on. As he reached his seat he expected a comment from Kirby's men, but he ignored them and sat down. He rubbed his brow as Woodward's comments whirled through his thoughts, but he couldn't decide whether the outlaw had played a trick on him before he died, or had admitted to something.

By the time the train pulled into Fall Creek he was no nearer to deciding the truth. So when the train lurched to a halt, he bit back his irritation, checked that nobody was waiting on the platform and alighted first.

Armstrong followed him out. While Jim stood on the platform he collected their horses. Then they waited for Marshal Kirby, who still leaned back in his seat, his hat covering his face.

Just as Jim was beginning to think that the lawmen wouldn't get off the train the deputies stood up one by one and, with surly gaits, alighted. Two of their number led their horses from the train and joined the others in lining up before the station house wall as the train took on water.

Jim and Armstrong stood apart from the group. Only when the conductor hollered that they were ready to move on out did Kirby raise his hat from his face and leave the car with a steady swagger.

He stood on the edge of the platform, facing away from the station house. The train pulled out, the wind whipping Kirby's long coat, but he set his feet wide apart and stood motionless. Jim and Armstrong walked to the end of the platform and, twenty yards to Kirby's side, rested their hands on their gunbelts.

Still the deputies waited, nonchalantly removing their hats and replacing them, or just tapping a raised foot against the station house wall. The only sound was distant birdcall. When the train disappeared into the dust and heat haze, Jim's impatience overcame his irritation.

He headed down the platform, past the line of deputies, who all regarded him with studied insolence. Nobody was on duty in the telegraph office, so he walked across the platform to stand beside Kirby.

"When are we heading to Clearwater?" he asked.

"My men will do what I tell them to do," Kirby said, facing the barren wilderness beyond the tracks. "You can go to hell."

"You must have seen the trouble I had on the train roof."

"Yeah."

"Well, those men were in Luther Wade's gang, and they're just a hint of what's waiting for us before we get back to Clearwater."

Kirby sneered. "If the likes of you defeated them, they don't worry me."

Jim took a deep breath. "Even so, remember I can be of use to you."

Kirby snapped an oath, but Jim turned and headed back across the platform to join Armstrong.

"Are we waiting?" Armstrong asked, his voice low. "Or are we hiding?"

Jim opened his mouth to answer, but lead tore into the wall above his head. He flinched away from the splinters and scrambled for his gun, while along the wall the deputies ripped out their guns and thundered gunfire in all directions.

Most of the deputies fanned out, but two of them stepped away from the wall to fire up at the roof. A cry emerged and a man who was edging over the apex tumbled down the roof to land on the platform.

The line of deputies blasted down at him, ensuring he was dead, as two deputies turned and hammered lead through the telegraph office door. For a moment, pained screeches from within drowned out the sound of thundering lead.

Marshal Kirby himself jumped off the edge of the platform to stand astride the tracks. He fired down the track at a tangle of rocks that was just beyond the platform. Although from his position Jim couldn't see anyone hiding there, Kirby still fired at the rocks.

On the third shot, two men made the mistake of bobbing up to return fire. Before either man could blast off a single shot, Kirby hammered a slug into the first man's stomach and into the second man's head.

The second man crumpled, but as the first man staggered away from the rocks, Kirby blasted a second shot into his side that spun him around and to the ground. Jim and Armstrong dashed out from the wall to search out other raiders as all around them the deputies maintained a furious barrage.

A second man rolled down from the roof,

clutching his chest. Two more gunshots thudded into him before he slammed to the ground. Another man made an abortive run around the side of the station house, but a hail of gunfire nearly tore him in two before he'd run three paces.

Two more men came out from behind an abandoned wagon to continue the ambush but, on seeing the sprawl of bodies, they panicked and hightailed it down the trail. Lead peppered their backs, knocking them to their knees and then to the ground.

A gunshot from behind winged past Jim's arm, but even as he turned to his attacker Kirby had blasted a shot between this man's eyes, wheeling him over the side of the platform and on to the tracks.

Three riders emerged from behind the scrub beside the station. Luther was in their midst but, on seeing the carnage, they swung their horses around and galloped away from the station.

Lead ripped into the trailing rider's back, tumbling him from his horse, and a speculative long shot winged the second man to the ground, leaving just Luther to run away. The gunfire ricochets echoed to silence and the only movements came from the tattered clothing of their attackers' bodies blowing in the breeze, the only sound the returning birdcall.

The deputies stood poised, each man facing in a different direction with their guns thrust out, awaiting any further attacks. Even though Jim had only known these men for an hour, he detected in their stances a confidence that suggested they didn't expect any of the raiders to still be capable of mounting an assault.

To a short nod from Kirby, they holstered their guns with a collective flourish and headed down the platform to their horses. Jim holstered his own gun and pulled up his sleeve to reveal that the bullet had torn through the cloth.

Kirby stopped beside him and smirked. "Yeah, you are of use to me. You gave them someone else to shoot at."

* * *

Outside the sheriff's office in Clearwater, only Marshal Kirby dismounted. The other deputies spread out in a sprawl that, to the casual viewer, would appear undisciplined. After spending several hours in their company on the quiet journey back to Clearwater, Jim could see the serious intent in the way they covered all possible directions from which an attack could come.

With the number of men they'd dispatched at Fall Creek, Jim reckoned that Luther was probably the only man out of his original gang of twenty who was still alive. Jim dismounted and hurried to reach the office before Kirby, but Kirby had already achieved a steady momentum. He brushed him aside and kicked open the office door.

"Hopeman, I've come for your man," he said, standing in the doorway.

Hopeman walked around to stand before Kirby. "I sure am glad you're here. Did you get any trouble on the way?"

Kirby chuckled. "I didn't, but Luther Wade's gang sure did. Now I haven't got time to waste. Where's the man who shot Benny Lawson?"

"Tyler Coleman's over here." Hopeman gestured to the corner cell.

In the cell Tyler yawned and leaned back against the wall with his hands clasped behind his head.

"I'm not interested in him," Kirby said, his voice cold and sneering as he walked across the office to stand in front of the corner cell. "I'm here to collect the man who shot Benny Lawson."

Hopeman furrowed his brow and when Jim shrugged, he pointed into the cell.

"This is him," he intoned.

Kirby shook his head and walked across the office to the doorway. He swung to a halt and waited with his head cocked to one side until Hopeman and Jim joined him.

"I don't appreciate taking journeys I don't need," he said.

"I still need you to take Tyler to trial."

"There will be no trial." Kirby gestured over his shoulder at Tyler. "That man didn't kill Benny Lawson."

TWELVE

"Dozens of people know he killed Benny," Jim said as he strode outside and stood on the boardwalk.

Kirby joined Jim and spat on the ground. "Any of those people care to explain themselves to me?"

Jim walked in a short circle on the boardwalk. "We don't have a live witness, but we have enough for you to take him to trial."

"If Judge Plummer weren't such a busy man he might enjoy hearing you explain yourself."

"He has to spend the time." Jim set his hands on his hips. "The court must decide the truth about who killed Benny."

"It must, but I know Tyler didn't kill him

because on the day *someone* killed Benny, Tyler was in jail in Green Valley, starting a five-year sentence for raiding Block Ridge's bank."

Jim winced and lowered his head. "Are you sure?"

"Yeah, because I arrested him two weeks before Benny died. For the next five years Tyler festered in jail." Kirby pointed through the open office door at the corner cell. "It's my guess Tyler completed his sentence a few weeks ago and was heading off to restart his worthless life, oblivious to your belief that he committed a murder."

"I don't understand this," Jim said, tipping back his hat. "People saw Tyler loitering around town right up until the raid and—"

"Will they swear on oath that they saw him?" Kirby snorted. "Or was it a typical frontier-town rumor?"

"I know how rumors start, but this was different. Too many people saw. . . ."

Jim sighed, shaking his head. He turned

to Hopeman for support, but Hopeman could only return a slow and sad shake of the head. When Jim gave a reluctant nod, Kirby sneered and turned to the Rusty Spur. He gestured for his men to join him.

"When you catch the man who did do it, tell me. Until then, you've got no reason to hold Tyler, and I've got no reason to waste my time talking to you."

* * *

Ten miles out of Clearwater Hopeman pulled the wagon to a halt. Hopeman rolled into the back of the wagon and removed the canvas he'd thrown over the bottom of the wagon to reveal the bound and hooded man beneath.

He hunkered down beside him and removed the hood to reveal Tyler, who cringed, his eyes narrowed against the brightness. Still staying quiet, Hopeman unlocked Tyler's handcuffs and stood back, but Tyler stayed curled.

"Get up," Hopeman said.

"I'm not making this easy for you," Tyler said, a tremor in his voice. He coughed and continued with a firmer voice. "I'm an innocent man and you've got no right lynching me."

"I'm not lynching you. I'm letting you go."

"I don't believe that. You hooded me and dragged me out of town."

"I did. Even if I know you're innocent, plenty more in Clearwater won't believe it. I've taken you out of town without anyone noticing. By the time anyone does notice, you'd better be long gone."

Tyler rolled to his knees and appraised his horse, Jim and Hopeman in turn, and then the deserted trail. He shrugged and jumped down from the back of the wagon.

"This is some kind of trick, isn't it?" he said, stretching. "You're raising my hopes, but then you'll take it all away."

"It's no trick. Marshal Kirby spoke up for you. He told us you were in jail when Benny Lawson died."

Tyler shrugged, so Hopeman rolled into the front of the wagon and raised the reins.

Tyler kicked at the dirt. "What about—?"

"Tyler, I don't know what you're trying to gain out of this situation, but it won't work," Hopeman snapped, leaning forward in the seat. "I made a mistake when I arrested you. I've put that right."

Tyler walked around on the spot. "I'm not looking for no gain. I just want to leave Clearwater alive."

"You've done that." Hopeman pointed down the trail. "So just get on your horse, ride away and don't ever return to my town."

Tyler took his horse's reins and faced Hopeman.

"What about an apology?"

Hopeman snorted. He shook the reins and hurried the wagon away. Jim stayed back, wondering how he could question Tyler about Zelma without alerting Hopeman, but when Tyler just mounted his horse and galloped away, he turned and hurried his horse on to flank Hopeman's wagon. For the next five miles the lawmen rode in silence, but on the edge of Caleb Lawson's land, Hopeman drew the wagon to a halt.

"Jim, the new investigation into Benny's murder starts tonight," he said, his shoulders slumping.

"I'm obliged, but aside from finding Luther, I don't know where to start."

"We'll worry about that later. Now I have to explain to your father that I had to let Tyler go. I'd prefer him to hear it from me first – and alone." Hopeman sighed. "I reckon if you tried to explain it to him it could be another five years before he'd speak to you again."

"I reckon so, too."

Jim flashed an encouraging smile and kept his horse back as Hopeman headed off toward Caleb's ranch. Jim waited until Hopeman was too far away to tell where he was going if he looked back, and then turned and headed off down the trail.

He rode northward and away from

Clearwater. He maintained a steady pace and within thirty minutes, he reached the spot where Hopeman had freed Tyler. Tyler had gone, but he searched for his tracks and, as there had been few travelers down this trail, picked them up with some ease.

At a fair pace he followed them and, within the hour and twenty miles out of Clearwater, he approached a lone rider heading away. Jim hurried, but when he was 200 yards back, the rider sped up.

By now Jim had confirmed that the rider was Tyler. He hailed him, but this forced Tyler to gallop off. Jim had no choice but to settle in for the long pursuit. With the extra distance Jim's horse had traveled Tyler rapidly increased the gap, so when Tyler swung in an arc around a huge outcropping of rock, Jim drew his gun and fired over his head.

As the gunshot echoed back from the outcrop and the crag beyond, Tyler flinched. Jim fired again, his arm thrust high, clearly showing that he was only firing to attract his attention. This time, Tyler slowed to a halt and waited for Jim.

Even so, he backed away toward the outcrop, seemingly ready to go for cover if Jim's intentions weren't benign, and he raised a hand to order Jim to stop when he was fifty yards away.

"Why are you following me?" he called.

"I've got a question," Jim said, drawing his horse to a halt. "I just want to hear the truth about Benny, and about Luther and about Zel . . . about anything else you'd care to tell me."

Tyler snorted, but when Jim smiled he nudged his horse on to meet him.

"I'll say this once, and you'd better believe it because there isn't no more. I didn't kill Benny."

"I believe you now." Jim waited while Tyler heaved a sigh of relief. "Why does everyone reckon you did do it?"

"I've got no idea. There couldn't have been any witnesses because I never met him."

"There was one – Monty Elwood."

"Monty isn't a reliable witness," Tyler said.

"So you did know Monty."

Tyler sighed. "Deputy, I've got a long journey ahead of me and I haven't got the time to waste talking to you. So either arrest me or let me go, but either way, you won't ever prove I killed some man called Benny."

"When you speak of Benny," Jim snapped, "remember that he was my brother and his death killed my mother and destroyed my father's life."

Tyler winced and then lowered his head. "I understand your need to make someone pay, but I still can't help you."

"Then try this – I can help you avoid Luther, but I need to know the full story to do that."

"Monty reckoned that Caleb . . . your father owed him five hundred dollars," Tyler said, his voice more relaxed than before. "So Luther and me agreed to steal what he was owed, but we had to leave town and we never carried through with the raid. That's all I know."

Jim nodded. "Why has your friendship with Luther turned sour?"

Tyler licked his lips. "Men like him . . . like us don't need much of a reason."

"So you didn't know I wanted you for Benny's murder?"

"Nope. When I rode into Clearwater, I'd planned to hole up with my three hired hard-cases and wait for Luther to find me."

"Three?"

"You killed two in the Rusty Spur. I guess the third hightailed it out of town when he saw the trouble he was facing." Tyler shrugged. "Now I'm moving on before Luther finds me."

"Then you've got less to worry about than before. Marshal Kirby killed a lot of Luther's men."

"I'm obliged for the information." Tyler frowned. "Why are you helping me? I didn't kill your brother, but I haven't been on the right side of the law much in my life."

"I'll be honest with you. Luther knows

about the whereabouts of a woman." Jim searched Tyler's eyes, but they didn't flicker with any interest. "I reckon you know about her, too."

"Is that woman Zelma Hayden?" When Jim nodded, Tyler rubbed his chin. "Was that why Armstrong kidnapped me, but you brought me back?"

"Yeah."

"I guess I'm obliged to you." Tyler dismounted and walked toward Jim. He stopped in front of his horse, and when he spoke his voice had none of its former arrogance. "That must have been a hard decision."

Jim nodded and swung down from the saddle to stand beside Tyler.

"It was, but doing my duty has a limit. If you won't talk, when I question Luther about Benny's murder and Zelma's disappearance he might learn that you headed north when you left Clearwater."

Tyler snorted a laugh. "I can see he might do that."

"I have to know what happened to Zelma." Jim flashed a benign smile. "If I know she's alive, I've got no reason to mention anything about you to Luther."

"You've got a way of talking a man around to your way of thinking. So I'll tell you this: she's alive." Tyler flinched and his eyes flared as he jerked his head to the side. "You idiot! You don't have to find Luther. He's found us."

Jim turned. A rider was galloping toward them. He was still some distance away, but Jim narrowed his eyes and confirmed it was Luther. Tyler became more agitated as Luther approached and when he was twenty yards away, Luther drew his horse to a halt in a cloud of dust. Then he dismounted and stormed toward them.

"Luther, stop right there!" Jim said.

"Be quiet, Deputy," Luther said, as he stomped to a halt. "I have business with Tyler."

Jim shook his head and walked around to confront Luther, aiming to halt this showdown, but Tyler barged Jim aside.

"It was always coming to this, so back off, Deputy," he said.

Jim shook his head. "I want information on Zelma, and one of you will give it to me."

Luther snorted. "Whichever one of us is still alive in one minute will tell you."

Luther and Tyler faced each other, ignoring Jim. He took a step forward, meaning to end this confrontation before it started. Then the thought came that last night Armstrong had tried to make the difficult decision for him.

He had rejected the opportunity, but Tyler was no longer under arrest so he was no longer his responsibility. With a sigh of resignation he raised his hands and took a slow step backward.

With his acquiescence, the two men stood ten yards apart. Luther was rigid, his eyes blazing. Tyler stood casually with one leg thrust out and to the side, a smile playing on his lips. Luther snorted a deep breath, his right eye twitching as he appraised Tyler's unconcerned demeanor.

His hand shook with an uncontrolled tremor, but with a roll of his shoulders he got it under control and hunched down. Tyler snorted a chuckle. Then, with a steady hand, he drew his gun using just his extended fingers, and punched bullets out of his cartridge belt to load.

A sneer passed over Luther's face and his hand edged toward his gun. Five yards to Tyler's right Jim broke into a run. With his head down he barged into Tyler's side, knocking him over a moment before Luther drew his gun.

Luther fired and the gunshot whistled over his head, as both men went down heavily. Jim kept the roll going, dragging his Peacemaker from its holster as he tumbled. Luther still had time to blast another slug at them, but the shot whistled by Jim's sliding form.

Jim slid to a halt and, lying on his side, slammed a shot up into Luther's left arm. The blast swung Luther's arm up, half-spinning his body around. Luther staggered back a pace, but then righted himself and turned to fire down at Jim again.

Lead ripped into Luther's chest and wheeled him to the ground. He moved to get up, but a spasm contorted his face before his head slammed into the dirt. With his gun drawn Tyler walked to Luther's side. He felt his neck and nodded to Jim.

"I'm obliged," Tyler said. He held out a hand to help Jim to his feet. "I never thought a lawman would save my life."

"Don't get too pleased. I didn't shoot him."

"You didn't. . . ." Tyler snorted.

Jim rolled over. A line of riders was galloping down the trail. These men were heading directly toward them in a line with guns brandished. Tyler edged back and forth, but one of the riders fired and a slug tore past his head. With that, Tyler ran toward the outcrop.

THIRTEEN

As Tyler hurried away from Jim, the line of riders galloped around the outcrop and headed for the crag. Jim raised a hand to his brow to shield his eyes from the low sun and tried to discern who they were, but the men blasted a volley of lead.

The first slugs were high and cannoned into the outcrop behind him. The last slug tore through Jim's hat, and that was all the encouragement Jim needed to join Tyler in dashing for the rocky outcrop.

Gunfire tore at their heels, forcing the two men to sprint the last few yards and then fling their hands up as they leaped for cover. Both men rolled to a sprawling halt behind the nearest boulder and then extricated themselves from their tangle. Their attackers had gone to ground, but from the tendrils of smoke emerging from the crag to their side their location was obvious.

"Who are they?" Tyler asked.

"I don't know, but I've got news for you, Tyler. You aren't a popular person in Clearwater."

Tyler shrugged. "Then I guess I'm glad I've got the law on my side now, even if he is stupid enough to get followed."

Jim raised his head, but gunfire exploded into the rock before him, ripping shards into his face. He dropped to the ground.

"Quit complaining. They probably foll-owed Luther." Jim sighed. "But I'll protect you, as I always have."

"Even if you do, staying pinned down here won't do us no good. I reckon we have to make a move before they get settled. So, we ambush them." Tyler pointed to a huge rock projection, some fifty yards to their side. "You go for that rock and get a different angle on them. I'll cover you."

"Tyler, you don't give the orders here." Jim rubbed his chin and then pointed to the rock. "I'll go for that rock. You cover me."

Luther chuckled. "That seems a good plan."

On the count of three Jim rose up and charged for the rock. From behind, Tyler fired up at the crag, but their attackers still risked returning gunfire and plumes of dirt ripped around Jim as the slugs cannoned into the ground at his heels and into the outcrop at his side.

As Jim ran, gunsmoke rose from at least five positions on the crag beside them. Then he concentrated on his running and, with his head down, scrambled into a hollow set before the rock.

He hunkered down. Beside him, a small gully ran up the side of the outcrop with protecting boulders on either side. If he gained sufficient height, he reckoned he could get above the crag and perhaps gain an angle that'd reveal his attackers.

He bobbed up and blasted a volley of

gunfire at the men's position, suggesting he was settling in for a long siege. Then he ducked and, on hands and knees, crawled for the gully. More gunfire erupted, and this time it came from a new direction.

Jim wavered, and then scrambled back into the hollow. Systematic firing was ripping out. From the plumes of dirt rising on the crag, this person was helping him. Jim waved to Tyler, who returned a bemused shrug.

So Jim searched for the location of the shooter. With the echoes, it was hard to work out, but he reckoned the firing was coming from the top of the outcrop to his side. To get a clearer view he crawled back from the hollow and shuffled around the side of the rocky projection.

He craned his neck to examine the side of the outcrop. A shadow fell across the ground before him and it was growing. He turned around, and he faced the form of a man jumping down from the projection above him.

He just had time to throw up an arm in desperate defense, but then the man slammed into his side, knocking him over and banging his head on the ground. He floundered, winded, and before he could extricate himself, cold metal pressed into the back of his neck.

"Stay down, Deputy," a gruff voice ordered.

With no choice, Jim lay flat. Around him, gunfire exploded, but the sounds were intermittent. People shouted, Tyler included, and then another burst of gunfire, and then silence. Footfalls paced away from him and then lead tore into the earth beside his left ear.

Jim slammed his face into the dirt. Somebody shouted and hoofs thundered. This time Jim risked raising his head. The man who had jumped him had gone and out on the plains a line of riders was galloping down the trail toward Clearwater.

Fingering the sore spot on his head, Jim staggered to his feet, swayed and then used a hand on the rocky projection to right himself. He shuffled around the side of the projection and into the hollow, but still no gunfire arrived.

He moved out from the hollow and hurried to Tyler's position. He found a single spot of blood on the ground, and scuffed earth, perhaps from a struggle. A return to Clearwater to organize a rescue attempt was pressing, but somebody had tried to help him by firing down from the outcrop to his side.

Jim reckoned this was the third time in the last two days that an unknown person had helped him when he was in trouble. So Jim headed to the gully and, with his head down, climbed, gradually speeding as his grogginess receded.

He quickly gained enough height to reveal the surrounding area, but he was only interested in reaching the tangle of rocks that coated the apex of the outcrop. They were as barren and seemingly devoid of life as all the rocks on the outcrop were.

He circled around to keep out of sight of these rocks until the last moment. Then he stood up and in full view walked toward them. He still kept his gun holstered as he slowed to a halt and stood facing them, about twenty yards back.

For several minutes he listened for any noise above the gentle wind rustling past him. Then he heard a faint neighing coming from the other side of the outcrop. Jim smiled to himself and risked voicing the wild thought that he'd kept at bay since Max Malloy had uttered his bizarre last words in which he'd claimed that he was searching for Monty Elwood.

"Monty, come on out," he said.

He waited with his arms folded, but only heard the horse again.

"I know you're alive," he continued. "I know you feigned your own death. The only question on my mind is why."

For a minute he waited. Then a man stood up from behind the rocks. He was grizzled and old, but the eyes above the matted beard were lively, and it *was* Monty Elwood.

"How did you figure that out, Deputy?" he asked.

"Tyler's third hired gun saw you. You thought he was going to kill you because you'd claimed that Tyler killed my brother. So you shot him, swapped clothes and, with Gene's help, you've been lying low."

Monty nodded and walked out from behind the boulder and across the top of the outcrop until he stood before Jim.

"Am I under arrest?"

"Being alive isn't a crime, and as you've tried to save my life three times, I guess I've got time to hear your side of the story."

Monty spread his hands, signifying that Jim should consider him.

"I haven't got much to say other than I've been living on my wits. Now I don't want whiskey no more and I've got me some self-respect."

Jim chuckled on seeing Monty smile for the first time he could remember.

"I guess you have at that. Armstrong

McGiven gave me a hint of the man you once were, and perhaps you can be that man again." Jim removed the smile. "It still leaves the question of what happened five years ago."

Monty narrowed his eyes. "Are you sure you want to hear about that?"

"I've pieced together some truths." Jim walked in a circle, ending with him standing beside Monty and facing Clearwater. "My father owed you money so you hired Tyler and Luther to steal it back. When Sheriff Hopeman ran Luther out of town, Tyler didn't have the guts to act on his own. Then Max overheard your plan and went through with it himself."

Monty sighed. "That pretty much sums it up."

"So why didn't you tell everyone the truth straight away."

Monty patted Jim's shoulder. "Believe me. You don't want to know beyond the fact that Max stopped me."

Jim closed his eyes and took a deep

breath. "I've gathered that Zelma had something to do with it, but I have to know the truth."

For long moments Monty didn't reply and when he did, his voice was low and resigned.

"Zelma kept Caleb. . . ." Monty coughed. "She kept your father *occupied* while Max stole his money."

Jim blinked hard, his former grogginess returning to almost tumble him to his knees. He took deep breaths to calm himself.

"I can't believe that."

"I'm afraid so. Zelma wanted excitement and I guess helping Max provided that, but she regretted what she'd done and couldn't face you, so she left town."

"I'd have forgiven her," Jim said.

"She didn't know that. She pleaded with me to keep her secret, but Benny was all set to work it out. So I led him in the wrong direction and he got killed in Black Pass. Afterward, Max threatened to reveal Zelma's role if I talked. So I let Caleb persuade everyone that Tyler did it."

With a hand to his heart, Jim got his ragged breathing under control and turned to Monty.

"Who did kill Benny?"

"It wasn't Tyler, or Luther, or Max, or me." Monty flashed a smile. "And it wasn't Zelma."

Jim raised his eyebrows, but when Monty shrugged he laid a friendly hand on his shoulder.

"These secrets have nearly ruined you, but Max is dead now and you've got yourself a second chance. You won't sort out your life until you tell the full truth."

Monty nodded. "I will tell you, but only when Tyler is dead."

"I need to know now." Unbidden, Jim closed his hand, clamping it tight around Monty's shoulder and making him wince. "Benny was my brother."

"I know, but if I tell you, it'll help you save Tyler, and I can't let that happen. I was an honest man before Tyler persuaded me to steal." Monty shrugged out from Jim's grip and walked away to stand on the edge of the outcrop and face the plains. "Everything that happened is his fault, and when he's dead, we can all restart our lives."

Jim joined Monty on the edge of the outcrop. "We all make our own hells, and letting someone kill a man won't help any of us. Only I can choose to move on and forget Zelma. Only my father can forgive himself for cheating on my mother, and only *you* can tell the truth and regain your self-respect."

"Those were fine words, Deputy." Monty turned to Jim. "I'll wait out here until Tyler's dead. Then I'll return to Clearwater and restart my life."

For long moments Jim faced Monty and then nodded and headed down the outcrop. Once he was down on the plains, he mounted his horse and headed back to Clearwater at a gallop. As he rode, he accepted that he had to talk to Hopeman now.

What he would say refused to become any clearer on his long journey back. The sun was dipping toward the horizon when Jim rode into Clearwater. He dismounted outside the sheriff's office and went straight inside. Hopeman and Armstrong were drinking coffee.

"I've got something to tell you," Jim said, squaring up to Hopeman. "It isn't good."

Hopeman invited him to come closer, but Jim stood with an almost military bearing with his chin held aloft.

"Relax, Jim," Hopeman said. "Nothing you can say will be as bad as meeting Marshal Kirby."

Jim rolled his shoulders, but then relaxed his stance a mite. In the last hour, he'd thought about telling him many different versions of his actions over the last two days, but it was only when he faced the sheriff that he decided he had to provide the truth.

As briskly as he could he relayed his attempt to gain information about Zelma by going to Luther's camp, about the snippets of information he had learned about her, about his attempt to persuade Tyler to tell him what had happened, about the showdown he'd let Luther and Tyler have, and about his failure to stop somebody kidnapping Tyler.

Despite his resolution to tell the truth, Jim didn't mention Armstrong's attempt to free Tyler last night. As Monty's planned resurrection was something personal to Monty, he avoided mentioning that and instead relayed the information about Max's and Zelma's involvement in the events of five years ago as being his own supposition. Throughout, Hopeman remained tight-lipped.

"If you want to dismiss me, I'll under-stand," Jim said, ending his story.

"I can't say you did right, but you should have told me about Zelma."

Jim tipped back his hat as Armstrong headed toward the window, shaking his head.

"I couldn't. I didn't know if her disap-pearance was personal or official business. I had to piece together whether she was involved in Benny's murder before I said anything."

"You could have told me as a friend. I'd have understood." Hopeman waited until Jim nodded. Then he slapped his thighs and stood up. "I guess that isn't important now. We need to search for Tyler."

"Where?" Armstrong said from the window. "It'll be dark when we get to the crag and he'll be dead long before—"

The door crashed open and Deputy Newell dashed in, waving a slip of paper above his head.

"I've got news," he said between breathless gasps. "Marshal Kirby's sent a message to Fall Creek. He wants to know whether you need help with your prisoner."

"What prisoner?" Hopeman said.

"The message doesn't say," Newell said, shrugging. "It just reads—"

"Wait!"

Hopeman took the paper from Newell. He read it and passed the message to Jim, who confirmed that it was just as confusing as Newell had suggested.

"Marshal Kirby has only just left Clearwater," Jim said. "He couldn't have returned to Green Valley by now."

"Perhaps an earlier message got delayed and we've only just got it," Hopeman said.

"No," Newell said. "The message got sent this afternoon and knowing it was urgent—"

"Damnation," Hopeman said. He snatched the message from Jim, read it again and slapped his forehead. "I know what it means."

Hopeman walked to the window, crunched the paper into a tight ball and hurled it away. Jim considered the message and even though there was only one explanation for it, his guts rumbled with the terrible realization that the unlikely explanation was, in fact, the only explanation. He joined Hopeman.

"I know what it means, too," he said. "The man who ordered us to release Tyler wasn't Marshal Kirby."

FOURTEEN

"An outlaw wouldn't intercept a message meant for Marshal Kirby and then pose as him," Armstrong said as he joined Jim at the window.

"Luther's direct approach *is* more normal," Jim said.

"So Tyler's alibi is false, but who else would go to that much trouble?" Hopeman said.

Jim took a deep breath, the sharp intake making the other lawmen turn to him.

"I still think Tyler is innocent, but I reckon that bogus Marshal Kirby kidnapped him," he said.

"That's my guess, too."

"I know that for a fact." Jim sighed and

flashed an apologetic smile. "I didn't deliver your message yesterday. My father took it and as it turned out, he delivered a different message to a different person."

Hopeman nodded. "I guess it was inevitable he'd try to lynch Tyler. The only question is, where did he take him?"

Jim turned to the door. "I reckon we all know where that is."

* * *

Jim crawled to the edge of the slope. Down below in Black Pass was the tree that marked the spot where Benny had died.

"Are you sure this is the right place?" Armstrong asked.

"It's the only place where my father would want to lynch Tyler. We've just got to wait, and he'll come."

Armstrong pointed to the horizon, where deep red clouds surrounded the flattened orb of the sun.

"By sundown is my guess."

Hopeman nodded and, with Newell, took a position thirty yards to Jim's left while Jim and Armstrong shuffled to the edge of the pass and lay on their bellies.

"You were quiet when I told Hopeman about my suspicions," Jim said.

"I had nothing to add," Armstrong said.

"Not even about Monty?"

Armstrong shrugged. "He made me promise not to reveal that he was alive."

"I won't reveal that either, but once we've saved Tyler, he will tell me everything he knows about Benny's death, whether he wants to or not."

Armstrong nodded. "Do you think Tyler will tell you about Zelma?"

Jim slapped the rock before his face and then rubbed his chin.

"Maybe he will, but I've never had a proper answer from you on why you're so keen to help me locate her."

Armstrong's eyes darted around the pass below as he shrugged.

"Some of Monty has rubbed off on me,"

Armstrong said, his voice sounding hurt. "He'd do anything for a friend."

"So would I, but. . . ." Jim rubbed his brow, his mind whirling as he pieced together something that he now realized should have been obvious to him. He lowered his voice. "Zelma left town after Max robbed my father, but some people saw her leave with a traveling salesman, and that man was you."

Armstrong shrugged. "That's a big surmise."

"There's more. After you stole her away from me, she left you. You reckoned that Luther knew where she'd gone. So when you arrived in Clearwater you weren't here to attend Monty's funeral, you were following Luther in your quest to find her for yourself."

"That's a mighty fine story."

Jim jumped to his feet. "It isn't no story. It's the only possible explanation for your actions. Now tell me the truth, damn you."

Armstrong gulped as he fingered his

beard. "Then I guess I shouldn't deny it."

Jim set his hands on his hips and bent double. "Why not just tell me before?"

Armstrong rolled back on his haunches. He stood up and squared up to Jim.

"How can you tell a friend that you now love the woman he once loved?"

"You can't," Jim said. He raised his hands above his head, his outburst attracting Hopeman's and Newell's attention. "But lying was wrong."

"You're angry. I can see that, but—"

"I sure am!" Jim stabbed a firm finger at Armstrong's chest. "Why did you steal my woman?" Jim slammed his finger with more power, forcing Armstrong to back away a pace. He continued punctuating his points with more stabs. "Why did you return to taunt me? Why did you lie to me? Why did you steal my life?"

"I did none of those things." Armstrong snorted as Jim slammed his finger again. This time he raised a hand and grabbed Jim's. He twisted it down to his side and pushed Jim back a pace. A hint of anger flashed in his eyes. "Do you really want the truth?"

"Yeah," Jim said, squaring up to Armstrong. "Let me hear it."

"Then I'll tell you." Armstrong raised his eyebrows. "Zelma said you were boring. I gave her the excitement—"

"That's enough!" Jim said and charged Armstrong.

At full speed, he slammed into his ribs and knocked him back three paces before the two men tumbled to the ground. They tussled, anger fueling Jim's wild blows as he worked off his frustration of the last few days.

Before he could inflict any damage on Armstrong's body, Hopeman and Newell scurried along the top of the pass and dragged them apart.

"Stop that, Jim!" Hopeman said, taking a firm grip of Jim's arms. "You're a lawman, and we're trying to save a man from a lynching."

Jim struggled to free himself, but then stood tall and lunged at Armstrong. The blow whistled through the air and fell short.

"He stole my woman."

"If what you said is right, you'd already lost Zelma when she . . . she dallied with your father."

"I'd have forgiven her, and I've got every right to pound Armstrong's ugly hide into the ground."

"You have, but this isn't the right time." Hopeman swung Jim around to face him and clamped his hands on both shoulders. "Is it, Deputy?"

"I guess this isn't the best time to start a fight," Jim said.

With Jim's more conciliatory tone, Hopeman relaxed his grip, but Jim used the opportunity to hurl out his arms and throw the sheriff away from him. Then he turned around and stormed two long paces.

With Newell still holding Armstrong rigid, he slammed a firm blow to Armstrong's cheek. The blow rocked Armstrong's head to the side and was strong enough to tumble both Newell and Armstrong to the ground.

"Stop that!" Hopeman snapped, advancing on Jim from behind.

The blood was still boiling in Jim's head. He dragged Armstrong to his feet and, with a round-armed punch to the chin, grounded him, and then stood over him.

"If you reckon you're man enough to steal my woman, prove you've got the guts to fight for her."

"I've got the guts," Armstrong said, fingering a trickle of blood dribbling into his beard. "After all the trouble we've faced together, you know that."

"I just know I thought you were helping me because you were my friend, but you were just feeling guilty."

Armstrong shook his head. "Nothing you can say will make me fight you."

"Then try this: if life with you was so exciting, why isn't Zelma with you now?"

Armstrong's eyes blazed. With a huge roar he jumped to his feet and charged Jim. Bent double and leading with his shoulder, he hammered into Jim's waist. His solid force wheeled Jim back five paces until Jim's foot slipped and they both rolled over each other.

Jim heard Newell's and Hopeman's exasperated complaints, but his mind was oblivious to everything but trying to slug the man he'd thought was his friend into oblivion. He threw up berserk blow after berserk blow, Armstrong defending himself by throwing wild punch after wild punch back.

They rolled into a boulder, and then rolled back, dust flying around them as they fought. Armstrong got a firm grip of Jim's collar and, on his back, wheeled him over his head to land behind him. Jim lay winded, and when he staggered to his feet, Hopeman was stepping between them.

"Jim, they're coming," he said.

Jim still moved to push Hopeman aside, but Hopeman's words filtered through his anger-fueled mind and he lowered his fist, as did Armstrong. Below them, a troop of riders was heading into the pass.

At the front rode the bound and gagged Tyler. Armstrong and Jim dropped to the ground to take up their previous positions. Hopeman shook his head and joined Newell farther down the pass.

"Don't go thinking I'm finished with you," Jim said from the corner of his mouth.

Armstrong's mouth opened, but he bit back whatever he'd planned to say. Below them, Tyler was bound on a horse. At his side, Caleb had the horse on a tight rein, and following them was the bogus Marshal Kirby and his supposed deputies.

They pulled up before the solitary tree within the pass and Kirby helped Caleb to hurl a rope over the thickest branch. They secured it and then tied the end into a noose and dragged it over Tyler's head.

Then, in front of the horse, Caleb fell to his knees. He ranted and wailed. He shook his fist at Tyler. He berated Tyler with a stream of invective, but Tyler sat hunched over, seemingly beyond hope that Caleb would believe his story that he was innocent.

On the edge of the slope, the lawmen viewed the scene, confirming that it was exactly what it appeared to be. Then Jim slipped back from the edge to join Hopeman.

"I don't like the look of this," he said. "I reckon my father has finally lost his mind."

"He hasn't," Hopeman said and raised his eyebrows. "He's just angry, and when men are angry, they do wild things."

Feeling suitably chastised, Jim and Armstrong exchanged a frown and a shrug. Then Hopeman moved to stand up, but Jim shook his head and gestured for him to stay down. He stood up and took steady paces down the slope.

"Pa, give him up," he shouted.

Caleb continued to rant at Tyler, but Kirby hailed him and pointed up the slope. Caleb still vented his anger at Tyler and Kirby had to pull Caleb away from Tyler's horse and point him toward Jim.

Caleb winced. He lowered his head and

then shook his fist at Jim.

"Stay away, Jim," he roared, his voice echoing down the pass. "I'm handing out justice for Benny like you should have done."

"This isn't justice and if you kill a man in cold blood, you'll suffer the same fate. I don't want to lose another member of my family."

"You lost me five years ago."

Caleb walked around Tyler's horse with his hand raised and ready to slap its rump and chase it away from the tree. Jim winced and broke into a run down the slope. Kirby spat to the side and swung around, arcing his gun toward Jim.

In self-preservation, Jim dove to the ground as Kirby's first shot whistled over his tumbling form. Kirby blasted sustained gunfire, forcing Jim to scramble for cover on his knees behind the nearest rock.

Then his father called for Kirby to halt his onslaught and, by degrees, the gunfire petered out, but the gunfire had spooked

Tyler's horse and it was edging back and forth, straining the noose around Tyler's neck.

At the top of the slope Hopeman ordered Armstrong and Newell to aim for positions down the slope and closer to Tyler and Caleb. In a line, they ventured over the edge of the slope. Again, Kirby fired up at them, but this time Jim swung his gun on top of the rock and blasted covering gunfire.

When this forced Kirby and his men to scurry for cover behind the numerous boulders in the pass, he got to his feet, vaulted the rock before him and hurried down the slope. Kirby and his men took it in turns to bob up and hammer lead at him, but he thrust his head down and pounded down the slope as fast as he could, zigzagging every time he reckoned another shot was imminent.

Armstrong and Newell were ten paces behind him, while Hopeman scurried in a long arc to gain a position twenty yards to his left. Caleb was yelling at Kirby to desist, but Jim didn't put all his faith in his success.

Ten yards from the bottom of the pass, he dropped to the ground to skid on his belly, gaining the minimal cover of a hollow, the higher position keeping him from Kirby's view. There he lay, getting his breath. Then he bobbed up, but gunfire tore into the earth before his face and he ducked again.

"Enough, Pa," Jim shouted. "However much you hate Tyler, you can't control those hired guns, and I know you don't want to be responsible for my death."

"Then back off," Caleb said.

"I can't. I have to get justice for Benny." Jim took a deep breath. "Benny would have wanted proper justice in a real court, too. He respected the law and he died defending it."

"Don't speak to me about the law," Caleb said. "If you were half the man Benny was, you'd have caught Tyler five years ago."

"You're right. Benny would have made a better lawman than I could ever be."

Caleb slammed his hands on either side of his head and roared his frustration. His pained shout echoed back and forth across the pass and, when it faded to oblivion, he faced Jim.

"I'm sorry, Jim," he said. He raised his hand to slap Tyler's horse. "I have to do this."

"Don't. I know about Zelma." When Caleb flinched and lowered his hand, Jim lowered his voice. "I know you went with her. I know you're obsessed with killing Tyler to avoid facing the truth that your weakness lost you your money, and Benny died trying to get it back."

"You will not accuse me of that," Caleb said. He swung back his hand.

Hopeman rose up and fired a warning shot down the slope at him, but Kirby bobbed up and his gunfire forced Hopeman to dive for cover. Jim and Armstrong tried to return fire, but Kirby's men kept them pinned down with a barrage of gunfire.

Then gunfire exploded from farther down the pass as a lone rider headed into the pass, his gun thrust out and firing. The man blasted a high shot into the chest of one of Kirby's men which wheeled him over a boulder, and then a second shot that slammed another man to the dirt.

Caleb stood by the horse for a moment, and then dropped to the ground in self-preservation. Fifty yards back from the hanging-tree, the rider drew his horse to a halt, his gun raised and aimed at Caleb.

The sight of the old and grizzled rider made Jim smile. The rider was Monty Elwood.

FIFTEEN

"Monty, you're . . . you're alive," Caleb said.

"I am now," Monty said, roving his gun over the boulders behind which Kirby and his men were hiding. "Now step away from Tyler. He's guilty of just about everything a man can do, but he didn't kill your son."

Caleb blinked away his shock and, with a shake of his head, he regained his composure.

"I don't know what you're trying to prove with this trick," he snapped, pointing up at Monty. He got up on his feet and took a determined pace toward Tyler. "But I've waited five years to have my revenge on Tyler, and nobody can tell me he didn't kill Benny."

Monty edged his horse forward so that he was twenty yards from Caleb and level with Kirby. Caleb took another pace and raised his hand to slap the horse, but in response, Monty lowered his gun and flashed a smile, encouraging Caleb to lower his hand.

"I can. Tyler didn't kill Benny. The man who killed Benny *was* Benny. It was an accident."

Caleb stumbled back a pace. "You can't change your story now."

"I'm not. I never said it *was* Tyler. You put words into my mouth and I went along with them. It was better than telling the truth when Tyler would never return."

"Benny was a fine shot. He wouldn't shoot himself by accident."

"He did, and you have to accept that. You tell everybody that Benny would have achieved great things, but even great men learn from the stupid things they do when they're young. Benny didn't get the second chance to learn that a gun can be more dangerous to its owner than its target."

Caleb's gun fell from his slack fingers and he crumpled to his knees. He kneeled with his head bowed.

"What happened?" he said, his voice broken and defeated.

"Benny rode into the pass, his gun drawn. I told him to holster his gun until he saw trouble, but he saw trouble behind every boulder. He fired in all directions. Then he fell from his horse. Somehow, he shot himself in the leg. I never thought a man could bleed to death from a leg wound, but the blood kept gushing out."

"How can I trust you?"

"I've got nothing to gain from lying, and everything to gain by telling the truth."

Caleb bowed his head so deeply his forehead pressed to the dirt. A single sob escaped his lips. Then he raised his head, the fire that had burned in his eyes extinguished.

"Then I guess I've heard the truth. Jim's right. My weakness got Benny killed." He sighed. "This is over."

"Caleb, you paid us to complete a job," Kirby said from behind his covering boulder.

"I did, but I don't want that job done no more."

"You might not, but I lost good men over this."

Kirby rose up and scythed an arc of gunfire across Caleb's chest, staggering him back two paces and into Tyler's horse, clutching his stomach. As the horse jostled back and forth, the motion rocking Tyler to the extent of his noose, Monty roared his anger and charged Kirby's position.

Monty vaulted the boulder, forcing Kirby to throw himself flat, and drew his horse to a halt. He turned and galloped back at Kirby. Up the slope, Jim rocked back on his haunches, horrified by the sight of his father lying flat on his back, but he bit back his shock and jumped to his feet.

With his head down, he ran toward the bottom of the pass. Kirby still had two men and they stood up and fired up the slope. At

Jim's side, Armstrong and Newell also ran down the slope.

Hopeman was to his left. All the lawmen fired on the run, forcing Kirby's men to dive for cover. As Hopeman vaulted down to the pass's bottom, one of Kirby's men risked returning fire.

Jim dove to the ground, Armstrong and Newell also going to their knees. Hopeman stayed on his feet and the hail of gunfire ripped across his chest, wheeling him to the ground. Jim rolled over a shoulder and came up on his feet and firing on the run.

His first two shots were wild, but his next shot tore into the man who had shot Hopeman, slamming him on to his back. The man plowed through the dirt before coming to a halt, but from the ground, he hammered a high shot into Newell's chest, spinning the deputy to the ground.

Then he turned his gun toward Jim, but before he could fire, Jim planted a slug in the man's forehead. He sprinted toward the second man. Beside him, Monty was bearing down on Kirby.

On one knee, Kirby readied his aim and fired up. The blow skimmed past Monty's shoulder and forced him to duck and veer his horse away. By Tyler's horse, Caleb thrust up a hand and, with a weak and desperate shot, fired at Kirby.

The shot was wild, but it made Kirby flinch and, in that moment of indecision, Monty tore his horse to the side and bore down on him at a gallop. Monty hammered lead into Kirby's shoulder, knocking him into the boulder behind him.

With his back braced against the boulder Kirby stood upright and returned fire. From only yards away the lead sliced into his horse's neck and dragged a pained screech from the animal as it threw Monty to the ground.

To Jim's side Armstrong was running toward this fight and, as Kirby took careful aim at the sprawling Monty, Armstrong slammed lead into Kirby's belly, knocking him to the side. A second shot hammered him flat and a third shot ensured he'd never get up again.

Jim continued to advance on the sole standing man, but, after winging a shot past the man's head, his Peacemaker clicked with a fatal emptiness. The man grinned and steadied his aim on him, but then staggered back and around as lead ripped into his chest.

He fell to his knees, but as he forced his gun arm to rise, a second shot to the back keeled him over to slam his face into the dirt. Jim turned around. Armstrong was standing with his gun raised. Behind him, Monty was lying beside his horse, his gun trained on the shot man.

"I'm obliged," Jim said.

"That's no problem for a friend," Armstrong said.

"That's no problem for a man who attended my funeral," Monty said.

SIXTEEN

Jim hurried past Monty and Armstrong to his father's side. Caleb was sitting up, a hand clamped over his chest.

"The bullet's not in me," he grunted. "It busted a rib, but I'll be fine."

Jim nodded. "I'll get you back to Clearwater and get you fixed up."

Caleb flashed a smile through gritted teeth. "As I'm in some pain, I'd be obliged if you don't take too long getting Tyler out of that noose."

Tyler's horse was still spooked and jigging back and forth, forcing Tyler to strain in the saddle to avoid being torn away, so he got up and took the reins. He talked calmly to the horse, stilling it, while Armstrong untied the noose from the tree.

Tyler jumped down and, when Armstrong severed his bonds, rubbed his neck and gave a huge whoop. Jim didn't wait for his thanks and dashed around the pass checking that Kirby's men were as dead as he'd presumed.

Armstrong and Monty checked on Newell and Hopeman, confirming that they were dead, too. They stood over the bodies with their heads bowed, but with the urgency of returning his father to Clearwater, Jim ordered them to round up the horses. Then he hunkered down beside Caleb.

"I guess there'll be consequences," Caleb said. He flashed a weak smile. "Whatever happens, I'm sorry. I never thought you were a bad lawman for not finding Benny's killer. I just couldn't face you after I ruined all our lives by going with Zelma."

Jim shook his head. "I'm not interested in hearing about the past no more. I just want a future."

Caleb nodded and patted Jim's arm. "Then perhaps . . . perhaps you could come for dinner sometime and we can talk."

"I'd like that, but only on one condition." He waited until Caleb raised his eyebrows. "You explain everything to Ma."

Caleb snapped his eyes shut. "I can't do that."

"Just because she's dead, it doesn't mean you have to cut her out of your life. I visit her and Benny every week and tell them what I've been doing, and I know she'll forgive you."

Caleb opened his eyes and swiped away the moisture that was threatening to brim over, so to give his father a moment alone Jim stood up and turned. As Armstrong had already secured two horses and was leading them down the pass, Jim joined him.

"Are you and him fine now?" Armstrong asked.

"We will be."

Jim edged from foot to foot as he searched for the right words to apologize for his former anger, but Armstrong smiled and held his hands wide apart.

"If you want to hit me because I stole your woman, I won't fight you this time," he said. "I'm not angry no more."

Jim gestured at the slew of bodies. "Yeah. Fights like this make you realize who your real friends are."

"They sure do." Armstrong pointed over Jim's shoulder at Tyler, who was leading the horse on which Caleb had planned to hang him toward them. "What are you going to do about him?"

Jim turned to Tyler, a faint smile on his lips. "Yeah, what am I going to do about you?"

"Like I told you, I'm guilty of plenty of things, but I had nothing to do with what happened here," Tyler said.

"I know, but you do owe me the truth about Zelma." Jim pointed at Tyler. "After all the trouble I've gone through to keep you alive, you will tell me."

"I don't know much." Tyler flashed a smile and then gulped and lowered his voice to a whisper. "She left me."

"She left you?" Jim blurted. He slapped a hand to his face and regarded Armstrong through the splayed fingers. "Does Tyler mean that after you stole her off me, he stole her off you?"

"I didn't, but Woodward did," Tyler said before Armstrong could answer.

"Woodward!" Jim and Armstrong said together.

"Yeah," Tyler said. "She went from Armstrong to Woodward, and then from Woodward to Luther, and then from Luther to me. Why do you think Luther wanted to kill me?"

"Then she left you?" Jim asked as Monty led the remaining horses to the bottom of the pass.

"Yeah, she said life with me just wasn't exciting enough. The last I heard, she was heading north to Block Ridge." Tyler tipped his hat. "As that's all I can tell you, I reckon I'll leave now. Other people in Clearwater could still want to deliver justice to me."

"I guess they could, but I've done a lot to

keep you alive. Make my efforts mean something and stay out of trouble."

"I was trying to do that when I rode into Clearwater." Tyler mounted his horse and swung around to pass by them. "I'll try harder next time."

When Tyler had trotted past the hanging-tree, Jim went to Caleb's side. With Armstrong taking his father's left arm and Monty bustling around them, they levered him to his feet, and walked him to his horse.

"Were you two fighting over Zelma, too?" Caleb said as they stood him straight beside his horse.

"We were, but once you're in good hands, I'll buy him a whiskey to show we've got no hard feelings," Jim said.

Armstrong shook his head. "Thanks for the offer, but I'm moving on now I have the information I wanted."

Jim frowned, but then nodded. "That Zelma was heading north toward Block Ridge?"

"Yeah. Even after everything she's done, I

still want to find her, and I reckon this time, I'll—"

"But she left you," Jim blurted.

"Zelma's a beguiling woman." Armstrong's eyes glazed, perhaps with an old memory. "There's nothing you can say that will stop me trying to find her."

Monty coughed and patted Armstrong's shoulder, making him turn to him.

"What if I were to tell you that me and her once had something special going?" he said with a gap-toothed smile.

"You and her?" Armstrong said.

Monty shrugged. "Like you said: she was a beguiling woman, and with—"

"That's enough!" Armstrong said, slapping his hands over his ears. He lowered his head. Then he sighed and shared eye contact with Jim. "Come on, Jim. You were right. We've got some drinking to do to an old friend that we . . . that a lot us knew."

Jim nodded and, with that agreement, they levered Caleb on to his horse. Jim waited while Caleb sat tall and confirmed that he could ride, and then headed to his own horse. Tyler was now a half-mile away as he rode on to the plains. Tyler's long shadow played out beside him and his gait was slow, but Jim couldn't help but notice that he was heading north.

QUICK ON THE DRAW

Scott Connor

When prospector William Crowley found a fabulous diamond, he thought he'd made his fortune, but three months later he lost it in a poker game. William never saw his diamond again.

Fifteen years later William's son Jackson discovers that the diamond is again at stake in a poker game, this time presided over by the entrepreneur Meeker Trent. With the help of his father's old friends Finbar Stuart and Preston McBryde, Jackson vows to win it back.

But the game attracts a motley collection of card sharks and gunslingers, and they soon discover that winning the game will be only half the battle. The hardest task will be staying alive for long enough to leave the poker table.

Made in the USA
Las Vegas, NV
29 April 2023

71322407R00125